PLAYING FOR KEEPS

PLAYING
BOOK 1

LAINEY DAVIS

Copyright © 2025 by Lainey Davis

All rights reserved.

No part of this book may be reproduced in any form or by any electronic or mechanical means, including information storage and retrieval systems, without written permission from the author, except for the use of brief quotations in a book review.

Cover by Qamber Designs

Editing by Becky with Bookcase Media

ABOUT THE BOOK

As the rookie goalie for the Pittsburgh Fury, I have one job: keep my eye on the puck.

I finally made it to the pros, like my father before me, and I have to prove I belong here. But lately, I've been distracted.

There's this woman. I met her after a game in Vegas, and we got a little drunk—and married.

My new wife is stunning, a cellist whose music breaks down my defenses. Amazingly, she's moved to Pittsburgh to be with me and she even fits in with my rowdy family. Everything should be perfect.

But while I fight to keep my spot between the pipes, she's struggling to find a path away from her controlling family. And now, her father is feeding nasty rumors to the press and I think my coaches believe them. The team is icing me out.

Was this marriage a reckless gamble after all?

Playing for Keeps is a sizzling sports romance with a tight-knit hockey family, a marriage of convenience, and two people learning to trust their hearts.

PROLOGUE
GUNNAR

There's a boob in my hand. I'm pretty sure of it. My head is absolutely killing me, and I know opening my eyes will mean agony, but there's a warm globe of jiggly goodness in my hand. I squeeze it to double-check. Yes, definitely a boob.

But that means ... there's a woman in my bed with me. I open my eyes. Sun streams through the sheer inner curtains of the hotel room, which means I fell into bed without the wherewithal to close the heavy drapes.

I recover from the sun blindness and tilt my head just enough to see the lush, white body sprawled over mine. A thick thigh straddles my hairy legs—hers is smooth and bright in comparison. She isn't wearing pants but appears to have panties on. Okay, so we probably didn't bone. That's good.

Good lord, look at that ass, though. Why isn't my hand squeezing *that*?

I move my eyes up her body, further to the long tank top, the rounded swell of her belly pressed against mine. And then the boob, which has escaped over the neck of her tank top, into my palm. I can't see this woman's face because it's buried in my armpit, but a mess of brown curls slides along her back, my side, the entire bed.

My left arm is tucked under her, and I realize it's asleep. Way, way asleep. I can't even move my fingers.

I groan and disentangle myself, reluctantly letting go of the boob. It's a fantastic boob. I'd pat it in appreciation if my brain weren't coming on board and reminding me that I have no idea where the hell I am, what happened, or who is in this bed with me.

Once I'm free from this goddess beside me, I sit up and manually work the fingers of my left hand with my right. Blood starts to flow again, and it hurts as the sensation returns to my fingers and wrist. This better not mess up my game—wait. I had a game yesterday.

Shit. Yesterday was my professional debut. Preseason. Vegas. I groan. We lost by three.

The groan wakes the goddess, and she rolls over, then notices her boob flapping in the air conditioning and yelps, tucking it inside the tank top. I stare as she sits up. This woman is flawless. Absolutely captivating. She has huge, brown eyes, long lashes, bright pink pouty lips, and a round face flushed from sleeping against my furnace of a body. I know her...I think.

"What happened?" She blinks at me and rubs her eyes, like maybe I'm imaginary. We stare at one another for a few beats. I'm assuming she, too, is hungover from whatever happened after the Fury lost. I bring my hands up to rub my eyes, and something catches my eye on my left hand.

I'm wearing a black rubber ring on a very significant finger. I glance at the goddess. She's got a bright purple ring on the same digit.

Fully awake now, I leap out of bed, looking around for my pants—I apparently slept in just a pair of boxers. I spy all my clothes in a heap on the floor beside the round table inside the door to the room. There are all the usual things on a hotel table—a weird lamp with switches that take forever to figure out, an alarm clock, and a notepad. But … there's also a pile of paperwork and a small bouquet of flowers.

My partner in apparent crime is also on her feet, tugging on dark jeans that hug her curves almost enough to distract me from the situation at hand. She pulls a sweater over her head and leans toward the paper. Squinting, she reads and looks up at me. "Gunnar Stag?"

I nod.

"Um … I think maybe we got married?"

I'm across the room in one leap, snatching the paper from her hand. Sure enough, she holds a marriage certificate, uniting me in legally binding matrimony to Emerson Saltzer. I stand frozen in place, trying to wrap my hungover brain around all this, when I hear a persistent buzzing—my phone.

I groan, bend over, and pick it up from under a pile of socks. It's my agent. I wince and press the green icon to answer. Brian's voice shrieks through the phone, as loud as if I were broadcasting him on arena speakers. "G Stag, where the hell are you? We were supposed to have breakfast with the brand reps. Do you or do you not want me to make you rich?"

Emerson…my apparent wife…purses her lips as I stare at the phone in my hand. Brian continues, yelling, "Do you know what hoops I jumped through to get you on the list as an ambassador for that Children's Hospital? What did I tell you—kids and puppies, Gunnar. Oy vey, I hate Vegas. G Stag, are you there? Can you hear me?"

I clear my throat. "Loud and clear, Brian."

"Then why the fuck are you not in your hotel room? Why am I standing in a pile of hockey tape by a G Stag duffel bag and an empty bed?"

I scratch at the back of my neck, trying to figure out what to say to Brian. He represents many of the athletes in my family. He can't just call us by our last name, and I used to like how my brothers and I were G Stag, A Stag, and T Stag. Today, it sounds ominous.

"Hello? Gunnar? Talk to me, kid. What did you do?"

"Well, here's the thing." I sit in the chair by the table with the damning paperwork.

"Aw hell." I hear Brian shake a bottle of something—probably ibuprofen or antacid. I wonder if he'd bring me some. "Out with it. I'm calling my clean-up crew the instant we hang up. What did you do?"

I glance at Emerson, who is now fully dressed, including socks and Chucks, standing by the table with her hand on a giant black case of some sort. An instrument? I shake my head. "Brian, I think I got married last night."

CHAPTER 1
EMERSON

The final note of my sonata rings out against the antique tile. I close my eyes and sink into the vibrations, letting the sound envelope me as the warm cello caresses my shoulder. I open my eyes, a smile tugging the corners of my lips for the first time in months.

The music fades, and I return to awareness…just in time to hear a hiss and a familiar voice with nothing kind to say.

Maybe I wanted to get caught. Maybe I just liked the acoustics of the New Jersey Transit lobby in Penn Station. Maybe I was desperate for a change. Either way, I'm unsurprised when my father halts in his tracks in front of me, kicks my cello case full of coins, and begins belittling me in public.

"What in the hell do you think you're doing?" His neck is taut, tendons visible above his immaculate collar and bespoke suit. "Begging in public? Like a homeless person?" I can tell he's trying to keep his voice down, but again, the acoustics here are terrific. It's interesting that he begins to yell about me being an embarrassment when he is the one making a public scene. Nobody had their phones out recording when I sat in a corner playing quiet, soothing melodies as they rushed to and from their trains. Nobody called security on me.

Dad grabs my arm, and I wrench it out of his grasp, glaring at him. "You have no right to stop me." Only because of the look in his eyes and concern for my instrument do I bend over and begin to pack up. My father stands, hands on hips, glaring as he breathes through his nose like an enraged bull. Or what I imagine one would look like. I've lived in Manhattan my entire life. I don't exactly spend time at the rodeo. My mother's voice is always in my head, reinforcing the rules: *Our people don't go to the zoo, Emerson, and we certainly don't attend sporting events.*

But I could, I realize. I graduated from college a few months ago, and I'm supposed to be preparing for the opportunity of my life—the life my father envisioned. I'm meant to audition to play the violin in his orchestra—the New York Symphony. Very few women are chosen. I've come to realize that my father is facing increasing pressure from the media to improve the gender ratio in his old boys' club on stage. I'm expected to play for him, with a smile on my face.

I stand with my cello case, swinging the strap onto my back, and face him. "Dad. Nobody noticed me until you started—"

He grabs my shoulders and shakes me, hard. "*Everyone* noticed you. You are my daughter. You are known, Emerson." He seethes in front of me, and I realize he is capable of hurting me. I see him staring at the instrument on my back, one he has hated since I acquired it. Refined ladies do not play the cello, in his opinion. I've been groomed for the violin. I've been trotted around and presented to reporters by his side. A dynastic duo, they call us. Musical genius Chaz Saltzer and his lesser-genius daughter, no name necessary in many of those articles.

I realize that this moment has been building in me for years. I am not happy in this life. I am not happy cramming myself into shapewear for cocktail dresses, appearing demure at fancy parties with donors. I am not happy playing only the style of music demanded by the maestro. And … I don't have to live this way.

Warmth washes over me as I make a decision. I flip my father the bird and slide into the first train I hear approaching.

It takes me a few minutes to catch my breath. I ignore the calls vibrating the phone in my purse, quickly paying for my ticket with an app when the conductor passes. I deboard at Secaucus Junction just as the Sky Train arrives en route to the airport. This feels like fate.

With my cell ringing insistently against my hip, I continue to ride the wave of good fortune as I ask the airline agent for the next flight I could feasibly catch.

I'm not destitute. I have a college degree, even if it is in violin performance, and I've never worked a real job or built any sort of marketable skills. I doubt my parents managed to put a hold on my credit card just yet, and I smile as the stoic agent books me on a flight to Vegas. I've never been.

Saltzers do not simply go to Vegas for the weekend. Oh, no.

Until now.

"You'll need to put that in oversized baggage," the agent says, pointing at the cello strapped to my back.

I recoil in horror at the thought of my gorgeous instrument banging around the belly of an airplane. She's not even in her hard case. "I can't do that," I insist, tapping my hands on the counter. "I'll have to buy her a ticket, too."

The agent's eyes fly wide at the suggestion.

"Can I not buy her a seat?" I'm sure I've heard of people doing this. I'm moments away from a nonstop flight across the country, and it's not a full one.

She bites her lip, starts typing, and then nods, eyebrows elevated like she's learned something new. "What, um, should I put for the name?"

And so, Baggage Saltzer and I head through security. Once on the plane, I silence my cell phone, tuck my purse under the seat in front of me, and settle in for a flight into the unknown.

I buckle my seatbelt and reach across the armrest to check on my beloved. Then, I accept a glass of water from the flight attendant and sleep the entire flight.

The first thing I should do is figure out where to stay now that I've arrived. Or even if I'm going to stay here. But when I exit the tram at the MGM resort, I notice a sign seeking live musicians. A day of reckoning that began with me busking at the train station, cussed out by my father in public, can now top off with me securing a gig playing background music for people eating a meal in between rounds at the blackjack table.

I'm in heaven.

The acoustics in The Velvet Mirage are divine, and

while I'm not quite dressed for glamour, I'm wearing my typical all black, and, as I explain to the manager, a musician's first job is to disappear into the surroundings.

And that's what I do. I sit in the corner of the stage surrounded by luxurious red curtains, playing whatever comes to mind in the intimate space with just a few tables, some sofas, and low lights. I start with some classical pieces I've memorized for the violin, transposing the music for cello. And then I try out some of the work I was testing at the train station. Mournful minor notes give way to hopeful, uplifting music that climbs and swells out of me. My fingers fly along the fingerboard, and my bow dances as the song seeps out of me. I've been dreaming of this piece, feeling it tug at me, unsure where to put it until this moment when it comes to life in this jazz bar.

I can imagine a life like this: making music for money in a gorgeous space. I let the music flow through me, both classical and original compositions. I am calm, even joyous, just making music—and getting paid!

The gig rate for tonight won't buy me a room here, but I'm not worried about that at the moment.

I'm deep in my element, experimenting with a piece that's been tickling the back of my mind for weeks. Now that I've broken free temporarily, the song comes to me fully formed. It seeps through my calloused fingertips as the staff delivers smoking, ornate cocktails.

It's all utter perfection until I lock eyes with a man so impossibly attractive I lose my place in the music.

CHAPTER 2
GUNNAR
LATER THAT DAY

"Yo, Gun, did you just puke in the sink?" Rogers, our starting center, pokes me with his glove, frowning as I wipe my mouth with the back of my wrist. I nod at him, and he groans. Soon, the entire Fury team is screaming at me to use the toilet next time I get nervous. I would have done that if I thought I could fit in the stall with my gear on.

My brothers bump me with their shoulders, flanking me as I hobble back to the bench on my skates. Those two were always going to be first-line players. The twins are mirror twins—one of them left-handed, one of them right-handed, and both massive. They operate on the ice as one being. Hardly anyone gets past them.

Me? I'm only starting because our legendary goalie tore something in his hip. Just like everything else in my life, this fell to me. Not because I earned it but because of circumstances outside my control.

"You gonna make it?" My brother Alder rests his forehead against mine and looks into my eyes.

I shove him away and nod as our coach starts banging

a clipboard against the wall, shooing us out of the locker room and onto the ice.

―――

The game is a blur ... except for each of the four times the Vegas Outlaws slide the biscuit past me.

After I shower, I want to go back to my hotel room and drain the mini bar, but I'm a professional now. I have to cram myself into a suit and shake hands with sponsors. I look at myself in the locker room mirror, adjust my tie, and smooth my hair. Guys are grumbling all around me. Nobody has said anything to me specifically.

We were expected to lose this game, but I still hate it. Vegas isn't usually in the preseason lineup for Pittsburgh, but we flew out here this year because our teams have the same title sponsor. For extra fun, we will be spending time with those Vegas Outlaw assholes after our loss, sucking up to our sneaker overlords.

But first I have to talk to the media about the loss I allowed.

"You got this, Gun." Tucker licks his index finger and tries to smooth out one of my eyebrows. I shove him away, but he just laughs. "Come on."

He and Alder push me toward the door. Alder snaps a pic to send to Mom and Dad, who were upset to miss our triple professional debut, but Mom had some bar association thing and wanted Dad at her side.

"G Stag! Hey!" My agent, Brian, snaps his fingers in my face, alerting me to the fact that he's probably been talking for a bit already.

"Sorry, Bri. What's that?"

He shakes his head. "I said don't leave after this. You and I have a very exciting date with a pen and paper."

Brian has been working to get me some endorsements. He's sort of the family agent, representing first my Uncle Hawk and then two of my cousins when they went pro for soccer. Now that he signed me and the twins, he's been trying to drum up fan support to pressure the management into giving me more ice time. He didn't use the phrase "capitalize on Grentley's injury," but I know damn well I need to shoot my shot right now. Or block every shot. Whatever.

I shake hands with all the suits and smile when someone walks past with a camera. Brian sticks to me closely, deflecting all questions about me taking over for Grentley and reminding the press that the post-game questions already happened. "We're here to celebrate shoes," he tells them, pointing down at my brothers' and my feet. We all look pretty fly in our Fury-branded special edition Adinas.

Eventually, Coach thanks everyone for attending, and we are set free. Most of the guys already have their wallets out, heading straight for the casino floors.

I'm not even sad about my agent dragging the Triple Stag off to a smaller bar inside the resort. It's some sort of speakeasy with velvet walls. Brian tries to order drinks for the twins and dumb-ass Tucker reminds him they're still not twenty-one.

I sink into my chair, sipping whatever whiskey cocktail Brian procured, paying half attention to him explaining how we're going to be the face of the new wing in the children's hospital back in Pittsburgh. "Be seen with injured children, gentlemen," Brian says.

"When the women swoon, they swoon loud. Nobody wants to bench the guy who's trending." He's got all kinds of admonishments about keeping up a clean-cut image, keeping our asses out of trouble and off social media.

None of that will be hard for me. I always kept my head down in college. Sure, I knew how to have a fun time, but I don't get sloppy drunk in public, I don't get in fights, and my parents raised me right when it comes to sex. Everybody leaves my bed happy, with clear expectations and a clean bill of health.

"Kids and puppies, Gunnar. That's how we get you to stay between the pipes." Brian clinks his glass against mine, and I nod, still simmering in post-game agony over coming in as a reserve goalie and then letting four past me.

I glance over Brian's shoulder when movement catches my eye on the stage, and I see the sexiest woman in the world playing music. Only then do I realize we haven't been listening to the radio or recorded tunes. This whole time, it's been this dark-haired goddess making all these delicious sounds. She's fair-skinned, curvy, and clearly passionate about her art because the face she's making is barely PG-13. Or maybe that's just my caveman response to her.

A cello rests against her body as she leans into the performance. Dim lights gleam off the redwood surface of the instrument, and her arm moves like a bird's wing as she works the strings. My mouth hangs open as I watch her eyes open and close, sometimes deep in concentration and sometimes wild with intensity. Her hair is tied over one shoulder, and her bare arms are toned and powerful.

By the time she stops playing, I'm already on my feet. Brian and my brothers look at me, then glance at the stage and start applauding awkwardly, but I stand there. I have to talk to her. I have to get her name, at least.

As Alder and Tucker lean into the Vegas atmosphere and start whistling, the rest of the patrons join in, cheering and whooping. The musician bows her head, sets her instrument on its side, and walks off the side of the stage to a waiting glass of water.

"Brian, I gotta go. Thank you for the drink and the hospital news." I set my glass down, and my brothers laugh as Brian mutters something about keeping myself out of trouble.

I adjust my collar as I walk toward the stage. I have to meet her. I don't even have time to come up with a line.

"Hey," I say, hands in my pockets. "You were amazing."

Her face shifts in surprise. She wasn't expecting anyone to approach her, I don't think, and she glances around. I know I'm a big guy. I don't want to intimidate her. "I'm Gunnar," I tell her, holding out a hand, hoping I managed to get the stink of my hockey gloves scrubbed off. "Can I buy you a drink?"

CHAPTER 3
EMERSON

The massive white guy approaching me right now is broad, thick, and tall enough that I have to crane my neck to see him. The rest of the room fades away until he's all I can see. It can't be healthy for one person to be this attractive. It's indecent, the way he looks in this suit.

I've seen a lot of men in suits.

The way this material clings to his shoulders, his watch twinkles at his cuff…the way everything tucks in at his waist and those pants curve around a perfectly round backside…it's utterly inappropriate.

I take a breath to center myself. I can hear some patrons talking about the men he arrived with. Over his shoulder, I see some approaching them with phones out. I hear the words "hockey players" and realize this trio are professional athletes.

I have less than zero desire to be in the background of someone's social media swoon over this guy, but actually, he doesn't appear to notice the buzz.

No, he's looking at me like I am the celebrity.

"You were amazing," he says, hands in his pockets

awkwardly, like I'm someone to be shy around. My eyes widen in surprise as I drink him in. He is objectively a perfect specimen of the human form. Even his neck has muscles. I guess all our necks have muscles, but his are *visible*.

"I'm Gunnar," he informs me after an awkward silence where I just drink water and stare at him. "Can I buy you a drink?"

I close my eyes and swallow the water. My set is technically done. As soon as the manager pays me, I am free as a bird. Refined conservatory girls do not go out for drinks with famous athletes in Las Vegas.

But I came here to escape all those rules, didn't I?

I'm about to nod yes to the hockey guy when the club manager approaches, fluttering his hands around a turban, the light glinting off the bangle at his wrist. "Emerson?"

I watch Gunnar learn my name and tuck it away with a smirk. I clear my throat and set down the water bottle. "Yep. I'm all set when you are."

The manager hands out a wad of cash, which should seem insulting but feels right considering the day I've had. "You were a real lifesaver for the dinner rush. Can we get your info for our sub list? I'd love to have you in our rotation. That was some really cool stuff you did. I never heard anyone play that sort of music on a cello."

I thank him, only briefly taking my eyes off Gunnar as he stands by, eavesdropping on this interaction. I settle up with the manager, give him my number, and finally turn to this handsome stranger. "You know what? I'd love a drink. Let me get my cello packed up. We'll have to bring her with me…"

"Her?" Gunnar follows me onto the stage, watching as I tuck the instrument into my case, securing the bow in the lid and ensuring all my other little parts and pieces are strapped tight.

I run a hand down the curve of the body. "Yeah, her. Look at that shape. No man looks like that."

He holds out a hand, and I'm not sure if he's helping me down the stage steps or trying to carry my cello. I slip the strap across my back and descend on my own, smiling. "Where should we go?"

Gunnar finds another bar not too far down the massive halls of the casino resort. This one has cheap well drinks, and I find myself agreeing to do a shot with him before we settle in with what he calls "sipping whiskey." I wouldn't know. I have very little experience with alcohol apart from the rare glass of wine at a function, for politeness.

"I loved how you moved with the music while you played," he tells me. "I felt like I knew what mood was coming based on whether you closed your eyes."

With his ice blue eyes boring into mine, this man is exploding my ideas of what a hockey player knows about music. The fact that he noticed the emotion and feel of my piece has me tingling everywhere. Nobody else in my universe has ever even commented when I've tried an original composition before.

"Thank you for noticing." I lean forward, elbows on the table, and clink my glass against his. "Not many people do."

He recoils in surprise. "That can't be right. Maybe you're just picking the wrong venues."

I bark out a laugh. "You have no idea how right you are about that." I take a bigger sip of the whiskey, feeling its warm spice of it all through my veins. "So why are you here with me and not at some strip club with your team?'

He arches a brow. "How do you know I have a team?"

I wince. Real smooth, Emerson. "I overheard everyone freaking out when you and those other guys came into the bar. You're hot stuff."

He sets his drink down and picks up his napkin, dabbing at the corner of his very full lips. I wonder why they're not scarred. I guess in my mind, hockey players are mauled-up franken-humans. Another pleasant misconception...

"I'm not hot anything, Emerson. Tonight was my first pro game, and I only played because our goalie wrecked his hip. Thanks to me, we lost by three."

I swirl the ice around in my glass. "I take it losing by three is bad?" I wince at his expression. "I'm not what you'd call a sports fan."

He smiles at that. "I guess that's another thing I like about you. I don't feel like I'm on display right now."

I chuckle and take another big sip. My body is feeling floaty now, my head swirling. "You're on display for sure. Every woman and half the men who walk by are drinking you in."

Gunnar leans toward me, sliding his glass away with his massive hand. "You feeling thirsty, Emerson?"

I swat at his hand and smile, taking the final sip of my drink. Leaning forward over the table, I can smell him: lime and cedar, whiskey and cinnamon. I stare into his eyes a bit and see some vulnerability in there. My whiskey-mind remembers his confession about his rough game, so I say, "I'm really sorry your debut was stressful." I brave running a finger along the back of his hand. "I might not know sports, but I'm very familiar with performance anxiety and the way it feels to overanalyze a bad night."

I watch him swallow, the beautiful muscles of his throat working, and then his jaw clenches before he nods. "Thanks." He furrows his brow, the sandy blond fuzz dipping toward those bright eyes. "You've played in public before? A lot?"

"Ha!" I reach for his whiskey and down it, surprising both of us. I sit back in my chair as Gunnar signals the server for another round of drinks. I wonder if he's feeling as buzzed as me, but I doubt it, considering he's probably got fifty pounds on me. And I'm no slim pixie, much to my mother's chagrin. "Gunnar, all I've ever done is play. My whole damn life was mapped out for me, but nobody ever bothered to ask me if I wanted to stick with that atlas."

"You don't want to play the cello?" He crosses his arms and leans back in his seat as well. He has already ditched the suit coat, draping it over the third chair at our table and covering half of my cello case. Gunnar has rolled up the sleeves of his dress shirt, revealing muscular forearms that seem unfair. These are not the forearms of a percussionist or viola player. These are the powerful arms of a man who could bench press a viola player.

I shake my brain away from staring and explain, "All I've ever wanted to do is play my cello. But I want to play my music, my way." I sigh. "I was doing that today, actually."

The server brings our replacement drinks, and Gunnar raises his glass in gratitude. "You sounded incredible. But I already mentioned that."

"Thank you. Today marks my big mutiny." He gestures for me to continue, and my words all seem to spill out at once. "My first act of rebellion was pawning my designer shoes to buy myself a cello."

Gunnar arches a brow, looking so handsome and intrigued. I smile and continue. "I took off my Prada Mary Janes and traded them for that gal over there. My parents were incensed. It's not a ladylike instrument, especially not when the player has to straddle the great wooden body like a lover." I watch as Gunnar's eyes shift at that. His jaw clenches. I have no experience with lovers, but I can tell the word is affecting him. I fiddle with my glass and lean closer, feeling bold. Maybe it's the liquor. "I was taught violin and flute—dainty instruments befitting the female child of a legendary conductor."

"Hmm," he nods. "You have a famous dad in the same industry." He raises his glass. "Now that's something I can relate to."

"Yeah." I smile at him and shrug. "Eventually, someone must have convinced my parents it was okay for me to have a side hobby...as if playing the cello were so very different from making other music. They constantly sneered at me, forced me to use a sound damper when I played in the apartment, but mostly ignored it as long as I went on dates with the appropriate sons of wealthy investors and wore my pearls to quartet performances."

Gunnar chuckles. "Pearls, eh?"

My phone starts vibrating in my bag again. I have no idea who is trying to reach me. I'm not feeling compelled to check. "Eventually, they'll find me and drag me back to the stuffy compositions by dead men. But today I just wanted to play my style, my way."

Gunnar looks alarmed. "Drag you? Who?" He sits up straighter, and I shake my head.

"Probably not physically drag me. But ..." I hesitate.

This is supposed to be carefree drinks. This guy doesn't want to hear my whole sad story. But then again, he was honest with me about his day. "I was performing in public this morning at Penn Station. My father saw me and blew a gasket." I don't tell Gunnar that the maestro called me worthless trash and an idiot. Even without these details, Gunnar seems upset. "Ordinarily, I sort of take it when he yells at me ... but today I figured, I have a college degree now. I am an adult. There's absolutely no reason I shouldn't turn around and just board the first train."

My date smiles, his face blooming with admiration. "That's kind of awesome. Wait. This was today?"

I nod. "Yeah. The train went to the airport, and the airplane went here." I finish my second glass of whiskey. Or is it my third? My speech is a little slower now, but so are my thoughts, and for that, I am grateful.

Gunnar laughs and takes a big swig of his drink, his eyes a bit glassy. I suppose he was drinking a little before introducing himself, and well, the two of us seem somewhat less than sober. "So, what comes next, Em?" He leans forward on his elbows, his face an inch from mine.

I purse my lips. "I have no idea." I lean closer to him. "What do you think I should do?"

Gunnar laughs and rubs the stubble on his cheek. "You could wait for that manager to call you. It seemed like you had a job offer there."

I shake my head. "No one wants to stay in Vegas. I certainly don't."

Nodding, he taps his fingers on the table. "I know I'm biased, but Pittsburgh is pretty nice. We have a symphony."

"A symphony is the last thing I want right now. No, thank you." When the server stops by offering glowing test tubes of neon liquid, my stomach protests, but my whiskey-fueled brain gets excited, and I clap my hands.

Gunnar pulls out some cash and procures two tubes, and we smile at one another over the blue drinks. "You could come and stay with me, though, while you figure out what's next. I have a big place, and I hate living alone."

I glance over at my cello. "You don't want me as a roommate."

His brows shoot up as he downs the drink. I follow suit and cough at the sickly sweet berry flavor. He says, "Don't tell me what I want, Emerson."

I clutch at my heart, hearing those words. "Oh, god, I'm acting like my father. You're absolutely right. I have no idea what you want."

He plucks the test tube from my hand and holds my fingers in his much-bigger, rough palms, as if I might be somehow included amongst the things Gunnar wants. His voice is like honey. "I'm serious, though. I hate living alone. I have a spare room, and Pittsburgh's a pretty cool city."

I smile at his offer. "I've only been to the ballet, years ago. I…" I don't want to admit that I performed in the pit because my father told me it was an important experience for my Juilliard application. I don't want to discuss doing the right thing all the time. "Tell me what's cool about it." I grab another tube from a server walking past and tip it down the hatch. Why stop making bad decisions now?

Gunnar smiles. "We have three rivers, for starters. You can ride a bike along the river all the way to D.C. if you want. Not that I ever went that far. And there's a bar near my place that used to be a brass foundry, and *then* it was a funeral home. And there's a space museum."

I laugh, surprised by his list. "I wasn't expecting that array of highlights."

He leans back in his seat, palms turned up. "What? You think I just care about bashing my brothers off the boards?"

I shrug. "I know it takes a lot of practice and dedication to be professional at something." I feel my tongue struggling to form all the words. "I'm glad you get to make time for that stuff."

He reaches for my hand. His skin feels like it's on fire, for sure. I glance down to check, wondering if there's a pharmacy nearby for my burns. But it's just two hands touching on the table. "Come back with me tomorrow. You need a place to stay while you figure things out. I need a roommate."

I frown. "Why do you hate living alone?"

Gunnar grins and shrugs. "I'm the middle of four kids. I've never even had my bedroom until now, and it's weird. Too quiet."

"That's a lot of family." He nods. I withdraw my hand and place it on my lap. "Say I come to Pittsburgh and crash at your place. What's in it for you?"

He jerks his head, a carefree gesture. "I get to know I helped a talented woman find her way."

The flush on my cheeks is unexpected, and I bring my palms up to feel my heated skin. "I would feel bad taking advantage," I tell him. "I'd be a bad roommate."

"We should just get married, then. You'd make a great wife." Gunnar laughs, and his blue eyes light up in the dim room. I don't know how many tubes we drank or how much sipping whiskey. He leans closer, closer, until his breath tickles my skin. "Fuck it, right?"

I laugh, but he isn't laughing. He's staring at me, his

blue eyes a bit out, thumb stroking mine. I feel every swipe of that digit deep in my core, like the vibrations of my instrument, only more sensual. I've never been very sexual, nor have I ever felt a burning physical desire. What he's suggesting feels ludicrous, impulsive, and utterly ridiculous. It's the exact opposite of what a refined, upper east side prodigy would do instead of showing up for her audition at the New York Symphony. I've had enough alcohol to know my family will explode in rage, yet not so much that it dampens my enjoyment of that thought. "Yeah," I tell him. "Fuck it."

CHAPTER 4
GUNNAR

Sunlight streams into the strange hotel room as Emerson and I sit on the bed, staring blankly at one another and sipping water from the smudged hotel glasses, until Brian bangs on the door and starts hollering for me to open up.

I do so, and he bursts in, shaking his head and popping Tums into his mouth. "G Stag. I saw you twelve hours ago, man." I don't mutter that it's been more like sixteen. I just wince. Brian gestures at me with his bottle of antacid. "I can't control things if you can't stop and think before you act, kid. You're like a damn puppy."

"Stop and think" has always been tricky for me. As a goalie, if I stop to think, I'm fucked. I operate off instinct and fast-twitch muscles. On the ice, I'm praised for acting before I think. Off the ice, well ... I do shit like anxiety-puke in the locker room sink and get married in Vegas.

Brian sinks onto the pull-out couch and presses a palm to his chest, closing his eyes. "Okay. We're going to fix this." He springs back to his feet and stares at Emerson.

"Tell me your name and if there is anything I should know about your family."

Emerson frowns and shares her name, then sighs and adds, "My father is the director of the New York City Symphony. He's going to really, really hate this." I know I don't know her well but I sense a little bit of smug excitement at the idea of pissing off her father. I can't relate because my parents are amazing, but I do love a good act of spite. I'm happy enough to help her with that if I remember correctly all the things she told me about him.

Brian nods and starts pacing. "I'm going to need my cleanup crew for this. When does the team fly back to Pittsburgh?" He looks at his watch. "Well, you missed that flight, G Stag."

My heart sinks at that news. Just what I need...to be perceived as a flake right when I need to be proving myself after a huge debut loss. "Shit."

"Yeah," Brian rolls his eyes.

My hungover brain shrinks from Brian's volume as he moans and groans, looking shit up on his phone and hollering when he sees photos of me on social media, staggering through the casino with my arm around Emerson's cello, which is strapped to her back. We look pretty cute together, I think. But I don't say that out loud because I value my life and trusted it to this agent.

Emerson finishes her water, rubs her temples, and raises her hand. Brian blinks at her and then gestures for her to speak. "Um, I was just curious why this is such a bad thing? We can probably get it annulled pretty easily, right?"

Brian sits down again, this time in the chair next to my wife. "Ms. Saltzer. Emerson. You were seen." He shows her an article from *Buzz Chat*, featuring a picture of us exiting the chapel with Emerson tossing a small bouquet at whoever took the photo. The headline proclaims, *DID HOCKEY HEIR MARRY MUSIC ROYALTY?* In another photo, I'm kissing her neck. I wish I could remember doing that and what she tasted like. I adjust myself in my seat, focusing on the sensation in my junk. I don't think I had sex last night. I'd feel it if I had. So at least I didn't do *that* while we were shitfaced.

Brian explains that he literally just signed the paperwork for me to be an ambassador for the children's hospital, about our strategic goal of presenting me to be photographed with kids and puppies to enhance my swoon factor and let the public pressure the Fury to start me on the reg.

Brian chugs another mouthful of Tums. "You grew up at a country club, right?" She nods, looking miserable about it. "Then you know why we can't just ignore this sort of thing." He gestures at her with the bottle. "And now you're the woman who took this stud off the market, so brace yourself for that backlash."

There's a knock at the hotel door, and Brian stands up to open it, revealing a pair of suited women wielding laptops. One appears to be East Asian, angry, and in charge, while the other has dark olive skin, deeply furrowed brows, and a couple of pencils tucked into her bun. The women nod briefly before placing their things on the hotel table, casting glances at me until I vacate the chair. Emerson follows suit, sitting beside me on the pullout couch as Brian engages in conversation with his "cleanup crew."

. . .

"Okay," says Brian a few minutes later, rubbing his palms together. "Here's what we're going to do."

He gestures toward one of the women—the angry one—who nods and says, "It was love at first sight. Devastatingly romantic." Her voice is utterly flat as she explains how Emerson and I knew we were destined for one another immediately.

"Like a movie. Very exciting," her companion asserts, equally without enthusiasm. "Look at them gazing at one another. They're insatiable." Brian squints over her shoulder at some images on a screen–a series of social media posts with hashtags and everything.

"Gunnerson?" I look up at Brian, confused. He shrugs.

The fixers nod. "We've decided that's your ship name. We've generated these images based on the ones already online, adjusting to bump up the palpable sexual tension between you."

My heart skips a few beats at this spy crap. The fixers have somehow created pages and pages of comments and reactions to news of my whirlwind romance. "Holy shit, Brian. How are you doing all this?" He waves a hand at me and then snaps his attention back to his crew.

"Right." The pencil-bun woman frowns and looks at her screen. "Emerson flew out here on a whim to audition for a new job at the Velvet Mirage when she met this guy. A romantic evening ensued, and like *Lady and the Tramp,* they fell ass over tits for each other."

The bossier fixer hums. "Emerson is obviously moving to Pittsburgh with her husband. She will be center ice at the Fury season opener and be at Gunnar's side for the children's hospital fundraising gala, perhaps volunteering to perform. This is to be discussed." She snaps her laptop closed and stands.

Brian sighs in relief and leans against the wall by the door. "This is why I pay top dollar for good people," he tells the room at large. Then, he turns to me and points a thick finger in my direction. "We're pivoting the strategy. Keep the kids, adopt the puppies this time. You are now a FAMILY MAN instead of a chick magnet. You are devastatingly romantic. You shower your wife with gifts and gestures. Get your act together, make arrangements to relocate your bride, and you'd better call your parents before they hear about this online and get insulted." Brian hesitates, chews his gum, and points at Emerson. "Your parents will probably freak out, too."

"They will," she says, but doesn't add anything further. She stares at her cello with an expression I don't know how to classify.

I'm probably supposed to be upset by the things Brian and his team are saying right now, but it doesn't feel like much of a lie to promise to act hot for Emerson Saltzer. But of course, we're strangers. It's not like she's going to run back to my house with me and become my instant soulmate. Without the encouragement of those blue neon drinks, things will probably feel awkward as hell. But we'll have to smile and ignore all that, I guess.

Brian and his crew leave the room in a cloud of mint gum fumes and antacid dust.

Emerson licks her lips and stands, refilling her water glass and chugging it down before turning to me. "Sooo, this is a lot."

I puff out a laugh. "Yes. Yes, it is." I lean forward with my elbows on my knees and rub my temples. My head is starting to feel better, but now I'm hungry and I have to try explaining this situation to my parents, which is pretty much the only thing worse than sucking at my job on an international stage.

Emerson's stomach growls, and I glance at her. "Let's order room service and make a plan."

She starts to protest and rummage around for her wallet. I sigh and grab the room phone, ordering a bunch of salads and sandwiches. I don't know what she eats, but I'm in season and have food rules. See, I'm thinking before I act...sort of. She presses her lips together, sitting opposite me at the small hotel table.

"Okay, so I have to fly back to Pittsburgh. I'm already going to get in trouble with the team for missing the flight." I look around. "This isn't even my hotel room. I have to find all my shit. Did I book this room for you?" She shrugs. "Well, you can stay as long as you want." I fish in my wallet and pull out my credit card. My signing bonus didn't quite get me the black card, but I've got a credit limit that is high enough to get her to Pittsburgh in comfort. "Take this. I'll write down my address. Our address, I guess...you can—"

"I don't need your money, and I don't need you to tell me what to do, okay? I'm here to get away from a man who uses his money and status to bully me into doing what he wants me to do." Emerson balls her hands into fists, and I want to rush over to her, wrap my arms around her, and apologize. This is the awkward part, happening already.

"I'm really sorry. That all came out wrong." I take a deep breath, and there's a knock at the door. I hold up a finger, greet the room service staff, and grab the tray from them, tossing a handful of bills into the person's hand before I set everything on the table.

I gesture for Emerson to choose and smile when she grabs a chicken sandwich and dives right in. I've always wanted to hang out with a woman who likes to eat as much as I do. I grab the turkey-BLT and eat half before admitting, "I've never done anything like this."

She laughs. "What? Got drunk and married? Me neither."

I tilt my head in acknowledgement. "Are you okay coming to Pittsburgh for a little while and rolling with Brian's plan? I can compensate you for your time."

She licks those lips again and moves to the sofa, tucking her thick legs under her and facing me. "Considering I just blew up my own life, I have nowhere to live and no job…yeah, Gunnar. I'll try this out for a bit. Honestly, it's a good idea to put physical distance between my parents and me anyway."

Relief washes over me, but it's short-lived because I still have to call my parents. Then she adds, "And I won't be taking your money."

I try not to growl. I want her to let me take care of her, but apparently, I can't force her to accept anything. I'm not sure why I feel so protective. "We can talk more about that later." I cram half a salad into my face and wash it down with more water. "I mentioned you'd have your own room, right? And your own bathroom. I don't want you to think I'm trying to seduce you or something." Her expression falls. "Shit. I didn't mean I don't *want* to seduce you. You're hot as hell, and I'd be–"

Emerson clears her throat. "Seduction isn't necessary."

I arch a brow, suddenly super turned on. "You don't want to be seduced?"

She laughs. "I think I can manage." I am going to have to follow up with her about that later, too. After waking up with all that boobage in my hand, I'm really hoping she's at least interested in fooling around once she knows me a little better. But maybe that's just the hangover brain talking.

Emerson and I make a plan for her to fly to Pittsburgh. I remind her several times that the fixers said I'm supposed to shower her with gifts. She lets me buy her ticket—and one for her cello to ride next to her. And then she leaves the room, promising to message me as soon as she lands. This gives me just enough time to call my parents before I get myself situated.

I take a leak, chug some more water, and lie back on the bed, feeling my heart pound behind my ribs. I pull up my phone and click the star next to Dad's name, knowing he will always answer, no matter what. I'm not even sure what time it is back home or if Mom is in court or something like that.

"Gunny!" Dad sounds excited, which kills me because I'm about to ruin his day. "Tough break last night, kiddo. Are you back in the 'burgh already? Want me to come over and talk it out with you?"

"Hey, Dad." I breathe in the silence for a minute and hear Dad pacing around, fidgeting. "So, um, that's not why I called."

"Oh. Okay…what then?" I hear voices…are the twins over at my parents' house already? "Hey, your brothers just got here. Why aren't you with them?"

"Dad, I need to tell you something." I close my eyes and pinch the bridge of my nose, waiting.

"Okay, let me duck out back." The porch door slides

open and shut on perpetually squeaky ball bearings. "Hit me, Gunny."

"Dad, I, um…I did it again."

"What's that, buddy?"

I close my eyes. "I acted without thinking."

"Hmm." His voice is reassuring. "Well, you know, that is a crucial part of goalie life. You gotta move that glove toward the puck before your brain registers that's what you're doing. You've always been my boy with the best quick-twitch muscle fibers and–"

"Dad," I interrupt. "I got married last night."

There's a clatter, and I'm sure Dad dropped his phone. I hear cursing, rustling, and then he is yelling. "You what? To who? Why?"

I bite my lip. This is the tricky part. "Her name is Emerson. She, um, plays the cello."

"So, you what? Got drunk and eloped in Vegas? Without the family?" His voice shakes, and I know I've wrecked him. Dad has been all in on the family since Mom got pregnant with my brother Odin. In fact, Dad retired from the pros to stay home with us while Mom ran for judge. Shutting him out of a marriage is the meanest thing I could do to him. My guts churn as he draws a deep breath. "This is unreal!"

Dad has shown up to every single hockey event, helping coach, throwing his name around, making connections. I'm not Gunnar Stag so much as I'm *Ty Stag's kid*. And now I've made a huge public mess and robbed my family of a chance to celebrate together. "I know I fucked up, okay? And the press is already all over it, and Brian is apoplectic, and you don't have to remind me that I'm a spastic fart, okay? I saw her playing music and bought her a bunch of drinks, and … we eloped."

I hear Dad breathing, slowly, steadily. I hear a bird chirping in the background, and then I hear his teeth click together. "I see," he breathes in some more. "When can we meet her?"

CHAPTER 5
EMERSON

Victor, the doorman in Gunnar's building, eyes me with curiosity. Which is fair because my clothes are two days old, and all I have is a cello and a purse. At least I fit in the tiny Uber that came to fetch me at the airport. Not sure how they would have picked up someone with any more luggage than this instrument.

The apartment is in a neighborhood called Lawrenceville, which my driver says is really hip and cool and *the place to be* for young people in Pittsburgh. And honestly, the building *is* incredible. I don't know what they mowed down to build it, but it's brand-new construction with a lounge, a game room, and a place to store kayaks. Kayaks! Nobody in Manhattan kept kayaks…at least nobody I ever had access to.

There's an ATM in the lobby, which strikes me as odd but certainly convenient. With trembling fingers, I insert my credit card, keying in a few hundred dollars I'll need for basic necessities after my Velvet Mirage payment. The screen flashes red: ACCOUNT ACCESS DENIED. I try a smaller amount—same message. My chest tightens as I attempt a quick twenty bucks. Nothing.

I glance around the fancy lobby, suddenly feeling like an imposter. Without access to my money, I'm exactly what my father called me - worthless. The credit card makes a satisfying sound as it hits the bottom of the trash can, but my hands won't stop shaking.

I spin on my heel and approach the desk. "You must be Victor." I force brightness into my voice. His eyebrows lift. "I'm Emerson. Gunnar Stag said he'd leave a key for me?"

When Victor lets me into the apartment, I thank him and look around. This whole adventure feels much less cool now that I'm here, with nothing, in a space that smells like the man I apparently married in a drunken bout of rebellion. Who gets married just to piss off their father?

Gunnar texted me that I should make myself at home and that the entire guest room is mine. He mentioned a third room that I could use for studio space if I wanted. There's a central living space with a kitchen along one wall and an island separating it from the living room. He's got a table and chairs, both heaped with neatly-folded laundry, and an overstuffed couch facing a massive television. A sliding door leads out to a balcony I can't quite see through the slatted blinds.

I peek in the first door down the hall, and it's heaped with random trophies and medals, presumably from Gunnar's hockey career. I set my cello next to a stack of wooden plaques and shut the door. I'll have to see about soundproofing the walls in there. I like the idea of having someplace to practice right here where I'm staying.

Apart from the whole "living with a stranger I

married" issue, the move to Pittsburgh actually seems like it could be good. There are a lot of arts and cultural opportunities here—a ballet, a symphony…opportunities my father would smile at. So, of course, I won't be pursuing them.

But I did spend time on the plane looking into other music organizations. There is an alternative group called String Fury. They play rock music on cellos and the upright bass. I'm practically salivating at the idea of connecting with them, volunteering for some of their educational programming, and teaching in their summer camps. I just have to figure out how to make it all happen.

The next door is a bathroom, while the one opposite it is clearly a guest room furnished as if it's a rental property —sparse, functional, and impersonal. I assume the last door at the end of the hall is the primary bedroom... Gunnar's space. I resist the urge to snoop in there and sniff his bath products.

Since I have nothing to unpack, I toss my purse on the dresser in my windowless guest room. I strip and hop into the shower in the hall bathroom, and as I'm drying off with a plush towel, unsure what clothes to put on, I hear the door open and close.

"Hello? Mrs. Stag?"

I poke my head in the hall and quickly wrap a towel around myself. "Don't call me that. I'm keeping my name."

He grins. "So, you made it." Gunnar scratches his neck, looking uncomfortable in jeans and a polo shirt with PITTSBURGH FURY embroidered around a hockey logo. I love the idea of us both working for organizations with Fury in the name. Not that I work for String Fury. Yet. But he should ditch the jeans and polo…gah! I cannot be ogling the professional athlete I married on a drunken whim. I cannot. As if I'd have any idea what to do with a man once he took off his clothes. Speaking of...

I step out of the bathroom, still in the towel. "I have an issue."

After Gunnar procures a pair of boxer briefs and a hoodie for me to wear, we sit on his couch to figure out how to create a starter wardrobe for me until I can send for some of my things from my parents' apartment in the city. I'm not entirely convinced my father won't have it all burned just to teach me a lesson. There's not really anything back there that I'd mourn if he did.

Gunnar slides a shiny silver laptop toward me and says his password is GOALIE, where the 'o' is a zero and the 'I' is an exclamation point. This is also the password for his Wi-Fi and, apparently, the mailbox downstairs. "You run a tight ship," I joke, shaking my head while pulling up a web browser.

"My cousins are always giving me shit about getting hacked. I figure I'll cross that bridge eventually." Gunnar looks over my shoulder, smelling excellent despite also having endured a cross-country flight. Maybe he showered at the hockey place. Perhaps he just always smells awesome. "My credit card should be saved in the checkout for Nordstrom." Gunnar reaches around me to type a login with one of his thick fingers. I need to stop staring at his hands.

I clear my throat. "You shop at Nordstrom?"

He chuckles. "They do alterations. I need special sizes for basically everything." He holds up a foot. "Even socks."

"How large *are* you?" I eye his bass-sized chest and thick thighs before my stomach starts flipping again, and I pull my eyes back to the computer screen.

"Wouldn't you like to know, wife?" Gunnar nudges me with his shoulder, and I shake my head. I've always assumed some combination of factors made it so I never thought too much about men's bodies or what I might do with one at my fingertips. Pressure to perfect my craft, concern about my parents, their insistence that I have the wrong body type for men of our social standing…it all added up to a total lack of interest. And now my body seems to want to make up for lost time with this stranger I married. I've been thinking impure thoughts about him, and they ramped up when he offered to seduce me, probably out of a sense of obligation. Gunnar mentions again that money is no object. I frown.

"I don't need to use your credit card. I told you I have the money from my Vegas gig." Not that it will last much longer.

"And I told you, you can use mine." But then his face softens, and he elaborates. "I don't want to control you, Emerson, that's not what I mean. You're helping me out big time. The least I can do is buy you some clothes."

He waggles his eyebrows, looking too adorable for me to stay upset about this. He's not wrong…I heard how his agent insisted we have to put on a big show about being wildly in love and that Gunnar is supposed to shower me with gifts. "Okay," I accept. He flashes dimples at me, and I wonder how much of a lie it is to claim infatuation with this man.

I order ten black shirts, ten pairs of my favorite black pants, and ten pairs of generic socks. I click over to order some underwear and bras, and when I glance at Gunnar, he's turned bright red and sprung up from the couch like it was on fire. "Something bite you?" I realize I enjoy teasing him. He's like a giant, friendly pit bull...all muscles and emotions.

He smirks at me. "Emerson, I'm going to let you be while you order what you need. I don't know about you, but I'm starving and going to get some food going." He walks toward the kitchen and halts. "Do you have allergies or anything?"

"I eat it all." Which can finally be true, with nobody here to sneer at my size or ask me if I really need a third bite of carbs. What will he cook for me? I don't care. And I love that. I smile as his face transforms into a more relaxed state. Gunnar clangs around the stove while I finish on the Nordstrom site and order some toiletries from a nearby drugstore. If this were New York, I'd walk to get them, but I splurge for same-day delivery since I have no idea how to navigate this city, which leads me to downloading a transit app and loading up a digital bus pass. I'm feeling pretty accomplished when the smell of onions, garlic, and cooking meat hits my senses. "Wow," I tell my husband, sliding onto a stool at the island in his kitchen. Our kitchen? "That smells amazing."

I realize I haven't eaten in a long time, and I am incredibly eager for Gunnar to finish plating the chicken, spinach, and mushrooms he has whipped into a fragrant tease. He slides me a fork and a heaping portion and then sits beside me with an even larger mountain of food on his plate. We eat ravenously for a few minutes—both of our hangovers gone just in time for jet lag to set in.

Gunnar swallows the last bite of his food and glances at my plate, where I've not made nearly as big of a dent. "I need to tell you about my family." He swirls a water glass in a circle, staring out the window at the city below.

"Okay. It sounded like your parents are not thrilled about this." I gesture between us.

He sighs. "It's not that at all. They'll love you." I know his words are generic, but something about the way he says it has me vibrating inside. What would it feel like for parents to dote on me rather than view me as an extension of their image? Gunnar reaches for my food when it's clear I'm not able to continue working on it. He takes another big bite and shakes his head. "The issue is that I got married without them there. The Stag family is … sort of aggressively affectionate." He rolls his eyes.

I purse my lips. "I have zero experience with that."

He pats my hand. "Well, buckle up, babe. You need to know that they're all going to want to meet you. And by want, I mean they're going to insert themselves and overwhelm you and possibly show up here with very little notice."

I dab at my mouth with a paper napkin from a stand at the edge of the counter and hand a napkin to Gunnar, who has now finished all remaining morsels of food from both our plates. "That doesn't sound too bad. I think I saw your brothers, right? So that's half the family."

Gunnar laughs, and my brows shoot up. He places a hand on mine and squeezes before hopping up to grab our empty plates. "Emerson. Sweetheart. That wasn't even all of my brothers. The Stag family moves in a giant herd—there are dozens of us."

I arch a brow and lean on my elbows as he starts washing dishes. I wriggle in my seat, fully aware that I'm wearing a pair of his underwear because that's all that would fit me, as this hulking man washes dishes after cooking for me. "Dozens? Seriously?"

Gunnar pauses, and I watch his lips move as he counts. "Yeah, including you. I think we are at two dozen, which is plural for dozens. Boom!"

My face must betray my hesitation at the idea of meeting multiple dozen Gunnar-sized people. I'm used to being scolded for my size, for taking up space when I'm meant to be serene and blend into the background. What would it be like actually to feel small in a room full of people? Do they all have Gunnar-sized personalities? He keeps scrubbing the pan and tells me his father has three brothers, each with a wife. "So that's eight. Then, Uncle Hawk's mom and her wife make ten adults."

"Aren't you an adult?" I flutter my eyelashes at him because, of course, I understand he's divvying up generations.

"Not quite," he insists. "Anyway, my family has four kids, plus six guy cousins and my cousin Birdie. And actually, my cousins Wes and Wyatt have serious girlfriends whom we consider family, which brings the total higher. Oh!" He claps and stares into the middle distance like he's thinking of something happy. "My brother Odin's keeping his lady, Thora. So, wifey, you're twenty-five."

"Twenty-five." I straighten my spine and press my palms into the counter. That's not just a guy and his parents. That's a whole web of family members now roped into this stunt. I press my lips together, thinking about what his agent told him about all the deals he's trying to secure. "Are you sure you want to do this? Are those endorsements really worth lying to dozens of Stags? How will we convince them that we're madly in love?"

Gunnar groans, slumps over the sink, and then lifts his

head to meet my eye. "I don't know, dude. Brian says it's important. The truth is, I just have this sense, and I need to see this through. Fuck it, right?"

I bite my lip because I did say that. Something is happening here, and it feels really huge, but I don't have the words to describe it. I'm attracted to Gunnar physically, without question. But I'm sheltered enough when it comes to men that I know I can't embarrass myself and suggest we try anything physical. The mere thought of presenting my awkward virginity to this virile specimen of sexuality leaves me nauseous.

Gunnar is still staring into my face, questioning. He says, "I don't think it'll be that hard to get them to think I'm hot for you, Emerson." He winks.

My eyes fly wide, and I shake my head. "That's not … we don't have to talk about that."

Gunnar brings the dish sponge to his chest like he's offering an oath. "You are absolutely safe with me, Emerson. But also, I meant what I said in Vegas. I'm happy to seduce you. Just say the word." When I scoff, his cheeks turn pink above his scruff. "Shit. Do you not like dudes?"

I puff out an incredulous sound. "I like men just fine." He makes a face I can only describe as sexy, and I groan. "Look, I'm super exhausted, and I've only known you a day I just … need to go to bed, I think."

He places his hands on the edge of the sink and nods. "Sleep tight, Emerson."

I stare at the man I married, watching as he finishes the dishes. "Night, Gunnar." I slide off the stool and walk into my new room, my body buzzing with confusion and anticipation.

CHAPTER 6
GUNNAR

Texts from my brother Odin start firing at me in the middle of the night. He must have woken up to an earful from our mom. He's in England for grad school because, I remind myself, he blew out his Achilles tendon, and his professional sports career was gone in a fraction of a second. This life is fleeting. The endorsements, the money, the opportunity to play pro hockey…it's fragile. Odin is the entire reason I left college early to go pro. His injury destroyed him emotionally, but it rattled our whole family. I need to take advantage of this career while I can because it could be gone tomorrow.

> ODIN
> You got married? Like legally married?
>
> ODIN
> To a human woman? Without introducing her to Mom and Dad? What the hell is wrong with you?
>
> ODIN
> Why didn't the twins stop you?

ODIN

> You better smooth this over with Mom.
> She can't keep calling me in the middle of
> the night. Thora is trying to sleep.

Oh, sure, I bet it's Thora bothered by all this. I power off my phone and throw it across the room. My sleep is so messed up, and I have goalie training before team practice in…well, in a few hours. I stare at the ceiling trying to come up with things to tell my parents about why Emerson and I are staying married, until my alarm goes off and I drag my bleary ass to shower.

I don't usually drink coffee, but I figure Emerson might, so I brew a pot and chug down some of that. Feeling more human, I make my way up to the practice facility north of the city. A lot of the guys live in the suburbs up here, but my family has always lived in the city. I can't imagine moving away from my family. I realize it's incredibly lucky that my hometown team picked me, but again, that's because my dad brought them more than one cup. I'm sure they're banking on his genes helping me more than they apparently do.

My commute is the opposite of most, so there isn't much traffic as I hop on the highway and think about my situation. It's pretty messy.

From what Emerson has told me about her family, she had a strict upbringing and didn't have the most loving home life. I'm hoping I can deflect some attention by talking about giving *her* space to figure out the next steps.

Mom's entire legal career has been dedicated to supporting women and families, which will probably work in my favor. I just need to drop a few hints about Emerson's dad shaking her shoulders at the train station, and Mom will have to be restrained from sending an assassin after him. Dad will be the one who holds Mom back.

Feeling secure in that plan, I head to the locker room, gear up, and meet Anton, our veteran Ukrainian goalie coach, along with Grentley—not dressed due to his hip injury but hovering to gloat or feel secure in his status as the real starting goalie. Or something.

Anton warms me up with a thousand low shots between sprints and on-ice stretches. Grentley glares from the side with his arms crossed, grunting every time I miss the puck. The hour passes quickly, and the rest of the team starts straggling onto the ice, which is when the trash talk begins in earnest.

Our center flicks the puck between my legs into the net. "Your wife teach you that move, Stag?"

A winger aims low, and I do the splits to save the shot. "I see your hips are nice and limber, Romeo."

Usually, the teasing is funny. Expected. My head is a mess today, and I know I shouldn't, but I'm taking it personally. When one of the twins reaches around the net from behind and sneaks the puck past my skate, I throw my helmet off and slam my brother into the boards.

His expression is typical: laughter. I can't even tell if it's Alder or Tucker at this point. I'm trying to yank his helmet off his dumb face when Coach blows a whistle, and I back off. "Gunnar. My office after."

The rest of practice is depressing. I feel like I'm skating through half-melted ice, trying to stop a hailstorm with a colander. I say nothing in the locker room while I change out of my gear and hurry through another shower, making sure to scrub hard enough to scour off the stench of my goalie pads. After practice, I usually have a whole moisturizing ritual, but that will have to wait. My mind immediately flicks to a fantasy of Emerson rubbing my salve into my thighs, and that will have to wait, too.

I make my way to Coach's office and sit waiting for him, my knee bouncing a thousand times a minute before he slides into his chair with a sigh. "What was that about, G Stag?"

I breathe in and out through my nose. "I'm not playing my best, Coach."

"Well, that's obvious. You've got bags under your eyes, and you're twitchy. Where's your focus?"

I shake my head. "I've got some personal stuff going on...and it's not an excuse but I slept for shit because my brother kept calling me from England."

He furrows his brow. "Which brother? There are more of you?" He mutters under his breath about thinking he had the whole family locked down, and I grin.

"My oldest brother doesn't play hockey, sir. He was upset about, you know, the marriage thing."

Coach frowns. "I saw something about that online. Or my daughter did." I tap my fingers on my knees, looking down at the silicone wedding band I have yet to remove. It already feels like it belongs on my hand. I briefly notice that my hand looks like my dad's hand now, with beat-up knuckles and a thick wedding band.

Coach taps his keyboard with his ring finger, which is similarly banded. "G Stag, I've been married for twenty-five years. Your home life is supposed to support your professional life, kid." I nod as he talks. "I don't need to explain the importance of mindset to you. You will leave this office and get your shit together, mentally. You will get back into your sleep routine, eat right, and show up to practice ready to perform. I don't want to have this conversation again."

When I don't say anything, he raises his eyebrows until I clear my throat. "Yes, sir. Understood."

Coach flicks a hand, dismissing me, and he's glowering at his computer monitor by the time I shuffle out the door.

I opt for a guided meditation audio on my drive home, repeating after the computerized voice that I will act and move with intention. Except, instead of thinking about my game, I'm imagining bringing Emerson to a family dinner and introducing her to all the Stags. I'm actually excited at the idea of showing her off to them. She's luscious, with curves for days and a dazzling smile she only lets out occasionally.

Thinking of her sitting in the Partners and Wives section of our games has me half hard, and imagining her with a G Stag jersey on takes me the rest of the way there.

I open the door to my—our—apartment and halt in my tracks when I hear music coming from the trophy room. She must be playing again.

I walk closer to the beautiful melody until I can just see through the open door. Emerson's seated on a bench in the middle of the room, where she cleared out a space among the stacks of plaques and medals I haven't yet taken the time to display properly. It's like my past is her audience as she wraps her legs around that beautiful, red instrument. She's wearing a sleeveless top, and I watch as one toned arm moves up and down the neck of the instrument and the other moves that hairy stick along the strings.

This isn't a gentle or delicate process. Emerson digs in, swaying as she moves, gripping the instrument with visible effort. But the sound seems effortless, big and deep, mournful. I didn't know I knew that word, but it's what I'm hearing as she coaxes sad notes that hang in the air or dance around the room. I become aware that I'm holding my breath, gripping the door frame as I watch my wife create something incredible.

She plays a final deep, long note and opens her eyes, locking onto mine, and her face transforms into a smile. She's happy to see me. I nearly faint, overcome by her talent and the fact that this stranger, my spouse, is glad that I'm nearby.

"Hey." She sets her cello down on its side and rests the stick thing on top of it. "How was your day?" Emerson crosses the room to me, fluffing her hair and rolling her shoulders. There's a faint sheen of sweat on her skin, like she'd been playing for hours. I wonder how salty she'd taste if I licked her.

But she's waiting for an answer, so I clear my throat, shake my head, and smile back at her. "Better now that I got to hear that. What was that song called?"

She opens her mouth to respond, but we're interrupted by a series of rapid-fire pings on my phone—texts with my parents' custom sound effect.

I hold up a finger apologetically and slide my phone from my pocket. I groan and show the screen to Emerson.

MOM
> I need to meet my daughter-in-law.

MOM
> You don't have a game on Sunday. Come to brunch.

MOM
> This isn't optional, Gunnar.

CHAPTER 7
EMERSON

Gunnar leaves before dawn every day this week, and I practice until he returns, smelling freshly showered, to cook us dinner. And then he talks to me until we go to bed in our separate rooms. It's a weird week, to be sure, but probably the most satisfying one I've spent… maybe ever. For the first time, I am fully in charge of how I spend my time. It's exhilarating.

Gunnar and I made a shared calendar, so I know all the dates of his games and travel. At first, I felt anxious seeing no Emerson items on our agenda, but once I added "cello practice" in red for multiple hours each day, I liked the look of our schedule.

I spent a little time obsessing over the String Fury music group, following them on social media, downloading their albums. This light stalking leads me to a website for a music academy that caters to kids who don't get access to lessons at school. The idea of a school with no music is so upsetting that I have to shut Gunnar's laptop and think about something else, but the Scale Up

Academy lingers in the back of my thoughts as something to explore more deeply.

I only leave the house a few times, seeing how far I can venture on foot. The city is not laid out in a grid, so I get turned around easily unless I can actually see the Allegheny River.

Which means it's the day before his family brunch, and I don't yet have a dress I can wear to the event. I didn't want to order anything like that online because dresses rarely fit my body in a flattering way.

So today is not a day to make music. Today is a day to figure out the damn bus system and find myself a dress. I've got in-laws to impress, dang it.

I consider asking someone at the desk on the ground floor of the building. Heck, I even consider stealing one of the kayaks from the wall racks and paddling around until I find a shop. But it all feels rather hopeless, and the websites for the public transit apps here confuse me to no end.

Everything in Manhattan was easy. Avenues run the length of the city. Streets are short across the width of the island. While I wouldn't say plus size boutiques are plentiful there, I could always find one pretty easily if I needed something to wear to an event.

I feel incredibly lonely here, alone in an unfamiliar city seemingly assembled by frantic goats. I can see another neighborhood atop a giant hill on one side of the street. Sprawling mansions cling to the wooded hills on the far side of the river, where Gunnar says the city ends and the suburbs begin. When I do venture out to the corner and glance up at the bus stop sign, I'm just confused all over again by the combinations of route names and letters that don't seem to align with the timetable I pulled up on my phone.

I've come to terms with using Gunnar's money for clothes and necessities to play the role of his infatuation. However, it just doesn't feel right to splurge on a car service or any extras when I don't even have a job on the horizon, or at least haven't identified what type of job I'd like.

Taking a deep breath, I decide I will just walk the length of Butler Street and find a shop that way. I wander in and out of cute boutiques selling skincare products and geodes. I pass yoga studios and candle-making businesses. But all the clothing stores are geared for tiny women. Thirty blocks past my new apartment building, and I haven't found a single piece of clothing that will fit me other than a lovely autumnal scarf, which I do buy because I need something to hide my face as I start the long slog home, crying a little bit and regretting my impulsive choices that brought me here.

I'm sweaty and tired, and when I can't even find shoes that fit me, I trudge back home empty-handed, apart from the scarf. I'm about to crawl into bed and hide when I hear Gunnar's voice behind me in the hallway on our floor. "Emerson? What's wrong?"

I stiffen. He hasn't seen my face, which I'm sure is splotchy, so I have no idea how he could tell something is wrong. I feel him step behind me and place a hand on my shoulder. "You seem upset. Can I help?"

I turn to face him, and he notices my tears. His mouth drops open. Then his lips press together in a firm line. "What happened? Who do I have to punch?"

I wave a hand, but a tear slips down my cheek, either

from relief or being overwhelmed. "It's dumb. I just couldn't figure out the bus, and this city's layout is so weird."

He reaches into his pocket for a key to the apartment and, opening it, steps inside and gestures for me to join him. "Why don't you just take my car? You can always drive the Benz if I've got the Rover."

I walk inside and set my bag on the counter, hesitating. "I don't drive," I tell him, patting the hard-won scarf into place on top of my bag. I turn to face him, gripping the counter behind me.

He scrunches his adorable face in confusion. "You don't drive … at all?"

I roll my eyes. "I grew up in the city, on the Upper East Side. I never learned to drive or ever thought I'd need to." I sigh and slump back against the counter. "But I really need a dress, and I don't even know where to find one in my size, let alone how to get to wherever that is."

Gunnar slides his gaze along my body and clears his throat. "Well, if you don't mind potentially being mobbed in the food court, I can take you to the mall. We can hook you up at Nordstrom." He grins hopefully.

My heart leaps a little at his offer. He does seem to truly like that store chain…for good reason. They are size inclusive. "That would be really great. Thank you."

He steps toward me. "Emerson. Of course. Let's go."

Buckled into the leather seat of his enormous SUV, I arrange my new scarf on my lap and smile at my husband as he navigates north. "We should figure some shit out before tomorrow anyway. This will give us time to talk."

He keeps his eyes on the road, easily crossing multiple lanes of traffic. I don't know why something as ordinary as driving seems sexy when he does it. I just need to accept that pretty much everything about Gunnar Stag is sexy.

"Right," I tell him. "We're madly in love, in public."

He nods. "And—sorry if this was overstepping—I told my family you're private because your dad is super pushy and a little mean."

I nod. "Well, all of that is accurate. Do you think they looked me up online?"

Gunnar spits out a giant laugh. "I'm certain they have a printed dossier all about you, Emerson Saltzer. My Uncle Tim is one of those cranky lawyer guys who knows everything about everyone. His mind is like a steel trap, which is great *and* terrible because he can always pull out facts to use as leverage."

"So, watch what I say around Uncle Tim. Got it."

Gunnar shakes his head. "You don't need to watch what you say. I want you to feel comfortable. I promise, everyone is really chill…they're just loud and nosy because they want to know everything about everyone they care about."

His words are like sparks from an exposed wire. "They care about me? They haven't even met me."

Gunnar bumps his turn signal and pulls into the mall parking lot. The gleaming entrance to Nordstrom shines bright before us, with the sunlight glinting off the windows. "Emerson. They're dying to smother you. You married their Gunny."

"Gunny?" I unbuckle when he puts the car in park. "They call you Gunny?"

He nods. "Gun. Gun-ster. G-Stag. Fart-ass. They'll want to give you a nickname, too."

I try to open the door, but he flies out of his side and races around to open my door for me with a grin. I accept his hand and climb down from the vehicle. "I don't really do nicknames," I explain.

He cackles. "Sorry, Salty. You're a hockey wife now. It comes with the territory."

CHAPTER 8
GUNNAR

"Salty?" Her facial expression is adorable.

I nod and gesture for her to head up the escalator, tugging my hat low so nobody notices me. "Salty. It suits you."

She laughs, and I melt a little. I've tried very hard to make it clear to her that I'm not going to pressure her into anything physical, but I'm super on board if she ever gets the urge. Because cheese and rice, this woman is every fantasy I ever had. She's rounded and soft, with long hair I want to bury my fingers in.

Emerson seems dead set on getting a new dress, and I'm happy to oblige, even if I feel like a bit of a slime ball imagining taking it off that delicious body of hers. She always wears black, which I think is part of the musician schtick, but once we're in the women's section, she walks toward a rack of bright green and blue dresses that seem really, really pretty.

"You should get them both," I whisper as she holds up a style in multiple colors. Her cheeks are pink, and she shakes her head, putting the blue one back and folding the green over her arm. Here, let me hold it for you." I take the dress and follow behind her as she looks around. It's only a matter of time before someone shows up to help us out, and I'm excited to insist the store give us the full personal shopper treatment.

"Hey, um, I wanted to check in with you about time frame for us," I tell her, glancing around to see if any of my alteration ladies are nearby. So far, I've been able to stay pretty incognito on this outing. But it's only a matter of time before I'm spotted, and it becomes impossible to browse casually.

Emerson peers up at me from behind a row of sunflower-patterned outfits that don't seem to suit her style at all. She sniffs and puts the florals back on the rack. "Brian mentioned something about six months," she says, pausing to glance around. "It'll take me that long to find a dress that fits."

I put a hand on her shoulder and look around, spotting an employee over by a wall of pink and red gowns. I beckon for her to follow me over there as I say, "I want you to stay as long as you want. But if you want to bail in six months, that's more than fair. We can just get divorced, I guess."

She purses her lips. "Why would we do that?" When I blink in confusion, she clarifies, "I mean, what reason will we give the press? You can't fake-cheat on me because of your image. And I'm not cheating on you. I mean, look at you."

I wink at her. "I'd never cheat on your fine ass, gorgeous." She swats at my arm. I shrug. "We can just have irreconcilable differences. You probably need to get back to New York for your music career. I'm never leaving the Fury if I can help it."

My heart squeezes at the thought of her returning to the city where her parents treat her like shit and yell at her in public. However, I also don't want to be part of a plan that prevents her from achieving her dreams as a musician. I listen to her play every day when I get home, and she doesn't know I'm there. She's absolutely incredible. She should be on every stage in the country, making grown men cry with her beautiful music.

I'm pulled from these thoughts by the arrival of Kamila, my favorite seamstress. "Mr. Stag!" She claps her dark sepia hands. "I almost didn't recognize you with your disguise. And who do we have here?"

I drape an arm around Emerson's shoulders. "Kamila, this is my wife, Emerson." I grin down at my confused bride. "This is the woman who will make sure you find the perfect dress and that it fits like a glove."

Within minutes, I'm relegated to an armchair outside a fancy suite of fitting rooms while Emerson is whisked away. I see Kamila's minions rushing in and out of the space with their arms full of fabric and I fuck around on my phone so I don't salivate at the thought of Emerson standing around in her underwear, trying on all those dresses.

Eventually, Kamila pokes her head around the corner. "Would you like to see our front runner for tomorrow?"

I hop out of the seat like it's sinking and rush through the door she holds open. "Definitely. What's tomorrow?"

This question rings in the air as I freeze, spying Emerson standing on a platform in a red dress so sexy I immediately grow hard and have to adjust my posture. The material is shiny, and the top fits her body so I can see every curve, including the one bare shoulder and two sexy calves peeping out below the flowy skirt. I claw at my throat, trying to find words. My voice comes out in a rasp. "That is fucking beautiful, Emerson."

She smiles shyly, turning and looking at her backside in the mirror, which means I see that heart shape reflected back at me in triplicate. It's all I can do not to rush forward and squeeze it. I'm sweating, impossibly turned on by the sight of my accidental bride. Kamila hands me a bottle of water, and I take it silently, chugging it down.

Emerson turns a few more times. "You don't think it's too casual for tomorrow?"

I take a step back and scratch at the back of my neck, trying to remember what I said we'd do tomorrow apart from a family meal. "Babe, I'm so sorry. I cannot remember what we're doing tomorrow."

She frowns. "Your family…brunch…"

My eyes fly wide, and I stare at Kamila. "You thought you needed this…" I gesture at her. "For my family?" Shaking my head, I fly forward and grab Emerson's hands, dropping the water bottle in the recycling bin on my way toward her. "Emerson, everyone will be wearing sweats. Soccer will be on the TV. People will wrestle." Her eyes flutter, and she seems to be on the verge of tears, laughter, or both. "Babe, this is a super casual family, I promise. But I want you to have that dress because I'm pretty sure it was made for you."

Kamila smiles and nods her head as if that settles the whole thing. I'm shooed back out of the room before Emerson can argue, and she appears a few minutes later back in her black everyday wear, with Kamila in tow, holding a garment bag. "Mr. Stag, we will have the others delivered after we complete the alterations. Is there any timeline for the dresses?"

I shake my head. "No timeline. Kamila, thank you for insisting that she get more than one." I flash her a full-dimple grin as Emerson seems frustrated that she wasn't able to talk her way out of receiving some pampering.

Kamila even offers to let us out a side door so we run less of a risk of a fan swarm. I reach for Emerson's hand, using the other to carry her garment bag. "I'm so sorry I didn't clarify that there wasn't a dress code for tomorrow," I tell her. Emerson shakes her head. She seems stiff...and I'm worried I messed up. "Talk to me, Salty. Tell me what you're thinking."

There's a small circle of women whispering to one another outside the fitting room suite. Word must have spread that a Fury player is here. I grin, wave briefly, and hurry to follow Kamila toward an employee area and out to the parking lot.

By the time we're back at the car, Emerson must have figured out how to verbalize her thoughts. "The idea of my family gathering in sweatpants is just ... inconceivable. I don't even know if my brother *owns* sweatpants. Is there a theme for tomorrow? An objective?"

"Objective? You mean other than meeting you and hanging out?" I blink at her as she climbs into the car and wait to close her door until she buckles her seatbelt.

When I'm settled in my side, she says, "That's another thing. My family doesn't just spend time together. There's always a donor we're wooing. A composer I'm supposed to impress..."

"Emerson." I turn on the car and flick the radio off so she can really hear me. "I don't know how else to explain this until you meet them ... but my family is going to be trying to impress *you*. *You* are the star of the show tomorrow, Salty."

She turns a charming shade of pink and glances at her lap. I swallow and merge onto the highway heading south toward our place. "So, what would you wear with that outfit in your other life? If you were going somewhere fancy?"

She leans an elbow on the window and appears to think about the question. "Uncomfortable shoes for sure. Makeup. Probably pearls."

I chuckle. "I can give you a pearl necklace, baby."

She seems to consider this like I was serious about it. "I don't have any of my jewelry here. Apart from this." She holds out her hand, staring at the silicone wedding band, which I notice she hasn't yet removed, either. "I would maybe like my pearls back, though. Do you really have some?"

The look on her face tells me she has no idea I was being a crude bastard, so I swallow and clear my throat. "I was being a dick. But I'll buy you anything you want. Seriously. Name it."

Emerson furrows her brow, and her nose gets a little wrinkle at the top. "Why did you say you had a pearl necklace?"

I sigh. "Look it up later. Then you'll know you married a caveman."

CHAPTER 9
EMERSON

I don't own sweatpants, but I feel fine in my regular black outfit, especially when Gunnar emerges from his bedroom in black sweats and some kind of sports jersey. I think it's a soccer one this time. He grins and points at me with a banana he grabs from the counter. "You ready for the antlers? Time to get pranced."

I groan. "You need to stop with the weird jokes."

"You love it," he says, opening the door and gesturing for me to exit first. He locks up the apartment, and I walk beside him toward the stairs, thinking that I genuinely enjoy his sense of humor. He's so easygoing. It's really refreshing to spend time with someone who has nothing to hide. Even though Gunnar claims he has everything to prove, he still manages to exude confidence and comfort.

"When are we getting you driving lessons, wife?" Gunnar gestures between his giant SUV and his sleek sports car. I shrug and point at the smaller car, which he unlocks and opens my door before I can get there.

"You're going to exhaust yourself always trying to do that." I huff and climb inside.

"I've got pro-athlete stamina, Emerson. Never." He hops into his seat and brings the engine purring to life. Gunnar hums along to the radio as he exits the parking garage, explaining that we are going to his aunt and uncle's house on the city's north side. "Uncle Thatcher is an artist, and Aunt Emma is an author, so their loft is extremely cool. Do you remember which little Stags are theirs?"

I nod my head. "Wes, his girlfriend is Cara. Both are pro soccer players. And Ricky…prefers to be called Rick. Still figuring shit out." I quote Gunnar's family summary with a smile on my face.

"You're good at this," Gunnar says, patting my knee before gripping the wheel to make a tight turn and rapid merge into four lanes of traffic.

"I, um, don't think I want to learn to drive in this kind of place." I gesture at all the signs whizzing past, the vehicles zooming past the sports stadiums and casino, along the winding river.

He hums, smiling. "I'll just have to haul you around myself then, won't I?"

After the mall last night, Gunnar and I talked about appearances. It makes sense that we should touch one another, and it wasn't until we mentioned it out loud that I realized how natural it feels to have him drape an arm around me sometimes or place a hand on the small of my back when he ushers me through a doorway. I can't tell if he's just being gentlemanly or if Gunnar just … clicks with my body somehow. I did not mention any of this to him or bring up my utter lack of sexual experience. I just agreed that he should, of course, squeeze my shoulder at the table and that I can tousle his shaggy curls if there's a lull in conversation.

I'm less comfortable thinking of his family researching mine. My parents and brother are easily searchable, too. But I suppose there's nothing to be done about the Stag family's perception of my family's online persona.

Gunnar parks outside a house that does indeed look cool. He squeezes my hand as he opens the front door and guides me up the steps to the living room. Turning his face toward the stairs, he shouts, "Yo, we're here. There better still be bacon."

I'm hit with a wall of sound as we enter a vast open room with high ceilings, windows overlooking the river, and a giant television mounted above a sofa big enough for fifteen large, athletic men. All of whom are yelling at the screen until they turn and greet Gunnar with sound effects.

A man with Gunnar's face pops up from the sofa and hurries over to us, and I stiffen, realizing that I'm going to be meeting Ty Stag, the father my husband was so worried about disappointing.

"Gunny!" The man's eyes crinkle at the corners, a smile taking up his entire face from neck to hairline, where some gray streaks only enhance his good looks.

"Are they here? Oh my god." I hear a woman's voice from another room and turn to see a dark-haired, statuesque woman in a soccer jersey and leggings rushing toward us. "You must be Emerson." She stops in front of me, looking like she was about to wrap her arms around me but held herself back.

I wave. "Hi, Mrs. Stag. I am glad to meet you finally."

"Mrs. Stag? Ha! That's my sister-in-law." She grins and reaches for my hand, squeezing in both of hers. "I kept my name. Juniper Jones. You can call me Juniper, though."

"Quit hogging her, JJ," says Gunnar's dad, who has

one giant arm around Gunnar and swats at his wife with the other. When Juniper releases my hand, he scoops it up and squeezes gently. "Tyrion Stag. Ty. Or you can call me Dad."

Juniper hits him in the ribs with her elbow. "Don't listen to him. Call him anything you want, dear. We are just so excited to know you better."

Her eyes are wet, like she might cry, and Ty kisses her on the cheek. He ruffles Gunnar's hair. "Gunny, you did so good, buddy. She's wonderful."

I bite my lip, not sure how to respond to this greeting. I'm rescued from my awkwardness by the door opening and someone else rushing into the house. "Am I late? Did I miss them?"

A woman climbs up the steps and beams. Her arms are full, but she drops her packages and pulls me in for a massive hug. "Oh, it's so good to have another woman here." She pulls back enough to look into my eyes but keeps her strong hands on my arms. "I'm Cara. I go with Wes. This place is a total sausage fest apart from the moms." She winks at Juniper, who laughs.

I remember Cara is a professional soccer player, and I am on the verge of feeling intimidated again when the living room crew bellows at the television. I glance around Gunnar and Ty to see a soccer game on, and a player with MOYER on his shirt is about to kick the ball at the goalkeeper. "Ooh," Cara whispers to me. "Wyatt's about to take a penalty. Hang on." I'm silent as the entire collection of gathered Stags stares at the screen. Wyatt takes a few steps back from the ball, then shuffles toward it, kicks it, and runs around screaming when it goes into the back of the net past the keeper's outstretched hands.

"That's my boy!" A slender man hops to his feet,

pumping his fists. While the room at large cheers, Cara taps my shoulder.

"Here," she says. "I brought you these so you would be ready." I see that she's holding a pile of athletic shirts. There's a soccer jersey that matches the one Gunnar is currently wearing, another one in black and gold, and then hockey jerseys in both black and white that say STAG on the back.

"These are for me?"

She nods. "You'll need them! Gunnar wasn't sure of your size, so sorry if they don't fit."

I'm deeply worried she's about to hand me tiny shirts, but I sigh in relief when I notice the XL tags. Cara rummages through the stack in her arms for a maroon jersey that says MOYER, like the athlete on the television, who I remember is Gunnar's cousin Wyatt. Cara stuffs the bundle of shirts into my arms. "Suit up, and let's get to the kitchen before these monsters eat all the food."

I pull on the jersey, which matches the one almost everyone else is wearing, and carry the stack with me as I follow Cara. We walk through a sunny dining room with a massive table into a spacious kitchen where a group of women drinks from champagne flutes.

"Oh, hello, you must be Emerson. Here, set those in a cubby." A woman with red hair takes the bundle from my arms and tucks it into a cubby by the door, where a pile of purses is heaped in a casual way that somehow sets me at ease. "Now," she continues. "Do you want the alcohol mimosa or the fizzy La Croix alternative?"

"Gosh, the mocktail sounds really good right now, actually."

I'm handed a drink, and Cara takes on the job of introducing me around the room. "Okay, Emerson, that was Emma, goes with Thatcher."

I nod. "Wes and Rick's mom."

Emma beams. "Gunnar filled you in!"

Cara snorts. "I bet he did. Anyway, that's Alice, Lucy, and you already met Juniper, right?"

Within minutes, the ladies are all sitting on stools around the kitchen island sipping fizzy drinks and tasting tiny bites of incredible food that Gunnar's chef-aunt Alice prepared. It's hard not to talk with my mouth full as each bite blossoms in my mouth like a celebration of flavor and texture. "I can't believe you did all this with just eggs and cheese, Alice. You are so talented."

"Why, thank you, dear. I've had lots of practice with this bunch."

At the mention of her family, they all seem to come into the kitchen at once, so I'm guessing the game ended. I'm soon lost in the din of happy people who genuinely enjoy each other's company, all eating little quiche bites, nuts, and breakfast meats as they stand.

Gunnar slides up behind my stool and presses a hand to the back of my neck, thumb rubbing soothingly as he dips his head low to ask, "You doing okay in here?"

I'm not pretending in the slightest when I grin at him. "I am fantastic."

He reaches toward my plate as if he's going to snatch the last bite of French toast, and I smack the back of his hand in a move that has his parents grinning. One of his brothers whoops. "Give him hell, Emerson."

I know Gunnar thinks he needs me to maintain some sort of public image, but honestly, I feel like I lucked into the deal of the century getting to tag along and be part of all this.

Emma eventually suggests we all relocate to the table so we can sit and talk more comfortably, and I make the mistake of checking my phone as I walk toward the dining room. I notice a series of increasingly angry messages from my father, asking when I'm going to stop this farce and come home for my audition.

> **DAD**
> Your mother can't show her face at the Met anymore. I hope you're satisfied with yourself.
>
> **DAD**
> Do you know how many young women would kill for the opportunity you're throwing away? You're not just disappointing me. You're taking someone else's chance.
>
> **DAD**
> I've told the symphony board you suffered a mental breakdown and are away seeking treatment. Your violin audition slot has been postponed for 30 days. When you're done with this tantrum, it's waiting for you. It's the only thing waiting for you.

I exhale a shaky breath and slide the phone back in my pocket, before taking a seat by a man who has never once spoken to me that way.

CHAPTER 10
GUNNAR

Things with my family and Emerson are going so much better than I thought they might. However, I'm not sure why I was worried. Emerson is awesome. She fits right in, and I even saw her laughing and joking around with my aunts in the kitchen.

If I didn't know this whole setup was a sham, I'd probably believe she's part of the family. We're a few hours into the meal, lounging around the table and talking. I have my arm over the back of her chair, allowing me to periodically run my fingers through her hair, which feels as silky and amazing against my rough skin as I imagined. However, having my arm on her chair means I can feel it vibrating each time she receives a text or notification from her phone in her pocket…which starts happening a lot more once Aunt Alice clears away the last of the serving platters.

"Hey." I lean in to whisper in case she doesn't want people to hear this. "Do you need to take a call? You're blowing up, babe."

She shakes her head, pressing her lips together in a way that makes me uneasy. Something's wrong. I don't get a chance to follow up because Dad slaps the table and says, "So, Gunny. Tell me what Brian has cooked up for you this week. Your brothers mentioned a certain sports drink…"

Emerson turns to look at me, her face brightening. I can't help the grin that's spreading across my own face. "Yeah, there's that, but he's also talking to some cereal folks, and I might get to do a milk ad."

Mom squeals. "With the little mustaches? I love those! Your father never got to do a milk ad." She jumps up and kisses me on the cheek. "We're so proud of you, sweetheart. All of this so early in your career. It's great."

Her words drill into me, splintering my bones with their emotional impact. This is why I'm keeping up the ruse, right? I didn't get here on my own two feet, but I can take these steps to make sure I have something of my own down the line. I've been watching Grentley. He's days away from a comeback, and then I'll be warming the bench if I don't step up.

I pull my mom in for a side hug and tell her, "I'm excited to get the ink dried. Thanks, Mom."

She doesn't step away but pats me on the head again and says, "We're not done talking about a proper wedding reception, though, young man. Count on it this summer, okay? After the season ends."

I should speak up and tell her we don't want anything like that, despite the futility of trying to talk this family out of a party once they get their mind set on it. But just then, Emerson's phone starts going crazy, and there's no way to ignore the beeps and vibrations shaking her chair.

Her cheeks flush adorably, and she reaches into her pocket. Then she drops the phone, hands shaking, and her face pales.

Concerned, I reach for the screen and see a headline preview. *MUSICIAN ON THE LAM. Emerson Saltzer, daughter of New York Symphony director Chaz Saltzer, has fled the classical scene to take up domestic duties at a hockey rink. Sources say she had a hasty marriage to goalie Gunnar Stag...*

A low whistle sounds over my shoulder, and I realize my brother is staring while I read Emerson's phone screen. "Hey, fucker. Get out of here." I shove Tucker back, but he already has his phone out, frowning at the screen.

"Shit, Emerson. I'm sorry they got to you. I hate these articles." Tucker shows the screen to Alder, who passes it to Wes and on down the line.

Dad's brow furrows. "What are they saying, son?"

I wave a hand, wanting to make sure Emerson is okay before I get into all this with my family. Growing up with the spotlight, we're used to junk press. From the look of my wife, she is definitely not used to being dragged through the wringer each time she goes out in public wearing the wrong outfit or gets too drunk at a party. "You want me to take you home?"

She nods almost imperceptibly, but I'm on my feet in an instant. Seeing the distress, Aunt Emma rushes to the kitchen cubbies and gathers Emerson's things, stuffing them in my arm in a flash. "Let us know what we can do, okay?" She jerks her head toward Uncle Tim, who is snoozing on the couch. "Your uncle can unleash his beast mode if you need."

"I know." I kiss her on the cheek and wave to the room at large. Mom mimes putting a phone to her ear, and I'm sure I'll be hearing from them all later, but right now, my main priority is my really upset fake-wife.

In the car, Emerson scrolls through her phone. I glance

over at screens full of messages, and then I hear the tiny metallic sounds of a voicemail.

A woman's voice spews hateful words, and I just catch enough snippets to learn it's Emerson's mother saying them. "...I suppose I should be grateful you didn't run off with that jazz musician from the Village. But really, Emerson. A hockey player?"

And then, "You know the Bergman's daughter just got first chair in Vienna. Meanwhile, you're what? Watching men beat each other with sticks? Darling, this is the sort of savage man you fuck to get it out of your system. You simply do not *marry* someone so far beneath you!"

And finally, "I always knew you'd use that cello to embarrass us, but I never thought you'd sink quite this low. Call me when you're done rebelling. And please, for heaven's sake, do not get yourself pregnant by that cretin."

Emerson knows I've heard. She turns to face me, shaking. "You don't have to listen to any of that, Salty. Nobody should talk to you that way."

I turn into the parking garage for our building and shut off the engine. Emerson is shaking, so I help her out of the car, up the stairs, and right into the kitchen for a glass of water. She sets her phone on the counter and stares at it. I wonder if the same words echo through her head as they do through mine. *Cretin. Rebelling. This is the sort of savage man you fuck.*

I take a big sip of my water and stare at her. "What do you want to do? I can take you to hit a heavy bag if you want to punch something. Or maybe you want to play your cello?" I don't want to sound pushy. I know Emerson finds her instrument relaxing, but the last thing I want is to sound like some other asshole demanding she perform for them.

"I don't know," she whispers. I keep sipping my water, crunching on the ice cubes. She smacks at her phone, and it slides down the counter, hitting the wall and bouncing to the floor on the living room side of the island. "I need to get out of my head."

I take a deep breath and set down the water glass, an idea forming. "Well." I step toward her, giving the ice cube one final crunch. "Since I'm supposed to be the sort of savage man you fuck for a good time…" Her nostrils flare, and her eyes spark with annoyance, but I finish my thought. "Do you want me to do that? Do you want me to fuck you, Emerson?"

CHAPTER 11
EMERSON

How on earth am I supposed to answer that question? Here stands Gunnar Stag looking sexy as sin in a T-shirt and sweatpants, all his muscles on display, sucking on an ice cube. My heart still pounds from my mother's hurtful words, so the lack of blood in my brain might explain what comes out of my mouth.

"I don't know how to do that."

I grip the edge of the counter behind me as Gunnar's brow furrows in confusion at my words. "What?"

I shake my head. "Intercourse…how would that work?" My cheeks heat at my use of that word, which I know sounds immature, but I just cannot bring myself to use the word Mom and Gunnar did. Not now. "It's probably a bad idea."

Gunnar picks his glass back up and slowly sips his water, taking a step closer to me. There is much less air now in the small kitchen. I watch his throat as he swallows the water, the muscles in his arm as he sets the glass back down. I didn't know I enjoyed looking at a throat until this instant. His voice is low as he says, "Salty, if it would take your mind off things, I'd happily lay you across the counter and lick your pussy."

My knees actually buckle, and I feel light-headed. My grip on the counter tightens, and I breathe in and out through my nose, trying to regain my composure. "That … isn't something I'd do."

Gunnar's head recoils in surprise. Maybe horror? He slouches toward me, voice still unbearably low. "You don't accept oral? Why?"

I risk releasing a hand from the counter to run it through my hair and push it away from my neck, which is very sweaty. I meet my husband's gaze and steel myself to explain to him, in summary, the entire problem that led me to this room. "I, um, have been very sheltered."

Gunnar shakes his head. "What I've seen from your family isn't shelter. There's no safety there from any storm. They are mean to you, Emerson. But what's that got to do with me licking your pussy?" Gunnar smirks and crosses his arms over his chest, leaning a hip against the silverware drawer.

I bite my lip because I hear it now—the judgment, the attitude, everything I said I wanted to escape, and everything that led to that stream of hatred from my parents. Their behavior extends beyond career choices and how I make music and has impacted how I relate to people. How do I break free?

Gunnar seems aligned with my thoughts. "I thought you wanted to get away from all that shit? Maybe you *need* a really good fuck."

Pressing his teeth into his lower lip as he pronounces the F on that last word will be an image that lives in my brain forever. As will the scent of his breath, since his face is closer to mine now. I swallow and grab for my hair, this time twirling it so I don't slap myself or pinch my arm to check whether I'm dreaming. "Well, how would it work?"

Gunnar spits out a laugh. "Emerson. Salty. It would work like a god damned dream. I would peel all that black clothing off you, spread you on the counter, and lick you until you come. And then I'd flip you over and plow you from behind and rub your clit until you come again." As he talks, he moves closer to me. "I've got an entire Safe and Satisfied basket on top of my fridge with every kind of lube you can think of. And I'd spread it all over my cock before I slide right inside you." I watch his chest expand with his breath, the subtle movements of his arms as he places them on either side of me, boxing me against the stove. He smells thick, if that makes sense, which it might not, because I'm drunk on the scent of cedar, lime, and laundry detergent. "Do you want that, Salty? Do you want your husband to fuck you?"

"I…" How can I explain to him that it's all too much, too fast? How do I ask him for just a little bit of his description? When he's clearly used to doing all that and more.

His description sounds fake. Like a fantasy of what sex is like. I've had a few nice boyfriends who were reasonably interesting on dates. I've dated flute players who I know have excellent dexterity and fine motor control, and I never knew how to take advantage of it. None of them made my body throb the way it is now, with Gunnar standing in front of me, hulking over me with his promises and his giant hands and inquisitive eyes. "Salty?" There's a question in his voice. I know that if I said no, he'd back away and go about his day. I also know he seems quite keen to try this ridiculous activity.

"What if I hate it?" I ask him again, knowing somehow

that that's not the problem. I will love what he proposes doing, and it will turn me into a different person—a person who just pursues pleasure, regardless of rules. And I hate how terrified that makes me.

He arches a brow. "Do you not enjoy having your pussy licked?"

I bite my lip. "I have never…tried that."

Gunnar swallows, and his eyes flash with something. Possession? Anger? His voice is a growl. "It will be my pleasure to fix that for you. But you tell me if I'm doing something you don't like, and I stop immediately. Okay?"

I nod, sure my spine is going to snap out of my body, and I will crumple to the ground if he keeps looking at me with that expression on his face.

"Salty, it has to be more than a nod." He steps back, and I feel the whoosh of air in between our bodies as he creates space. "Tell me, with words, if you want me to fuck you right now."

I could tell him no. I could take a shower, smash my phone, and play my cello until I work out all these emotions. But he smells so good, sexy with a hint of maple syrup from the breakfast I just enjoyed more than my entire four years of college, and I don't want to say no.

I … want to try what he's offering, but I'm worried the plowing portion will be too much.

"Can we just do the first part? Without the bending over?" My words are breathy and quiet, but his expression softens as soon as I utter them.

He rubs a hand down my cheek. "That sounds amazing," he whispers.

I frown. "How would that be amazing for you?"

Gunnar clutches at his chest. "Wife, I have been

dreaming of licking your pussy for days. I can't wait to taste you. If you want."

"Yes, please," I utter, and he chuckles.

He takes a step closer to me, arms still boxing me in again. I can feel a thick ridge pressed against my stomach and so much heat radiating from his body that I wonder if we somehow turned the oven on. "Which part, Salty? What do you want?"

"Um. What you said. With the counter and the licking. Please."

The instant the words leave my mouth, I'm hoisted into the air by a pair of solid arms. He spins us, setting me on the island and tugging at my shirt. Gunnar hisses in a breath when he pulls it up and over my head, revealing my very sensible black bra. I try to cover my stomach with my arm, but he shakes his head. "I wasn't done looking," he says, skating a palm up my side. I never show anyone my stomach. I'm used to being told to suck it in, make it smaller. But Gunnar stares at it now like it's a gift to behold.

He tugs me to the edge of the counter so I'm straddling his waist, pressed right against his shirt. I realize with a combination of horror and fascination that I'm wet, and this moisture will get on his clothes. "Mmm." He makes a sound of appreciation as he touches my boobs through my bra.

His thumbs circle my nipples through the fabric, and I gasp. It feels electric, with actual crackles and zings. Gunnar, studying my face, smirks a crooked little smile and licks his lips. "This is going to be awesome," he says, unhooking my bra with ease, tossing it behind me into the living room. And then his mouth is on my skin, hot and so wet. Without thinking, I bring my hands to his hair and press his head against my body as he sucks. And he groans! He liked that.

I yelp when he pinches my nipples and squeak when he orders me to lie back. The counter is cold against my bare back, but it warms quickly, or else I stop focusing on it as Gunnar pulls off my pants and my underwear, and then I'm absolutely naked while he's fully clothed, standing in between my legs, grinning. "Damn, Salty, you are so perfect. Just look at you."

I raise up on my forearms and look, trying to see what he sees. His hands are in constant motion, smoothing up and down my thighs, my stomach, my boobs. He starts murmuring, maybe to himself. "So soft," he says, kissing my inner thigh. "So lush." He is not so different from a musician, stroking his hands along my legs, bending my knees, and placing my feet on the edge of the counter. I'm spread impossibly wide, utterly indecent with my bottom at the edge of the counter and a massive hockey player staring into my crotch.

I wriggle and try to close my body, but Gunnar shakes his head and presses a hand to my belly to still me. "Show me," he says. And then his eyes darken, pupils enormous. He looks positively feral when he says, "Show me what's mine."

CHAPTER 12
GUNNAR

Emerson gulps at my possessive words, but I don't fucking care. I can barely contain myself as her scent invades my nostrils. She is utterly gorgeous, her curves on display just for me in my fucking kitchen, like the most gourmet meal I've ever been served.

When she lets her knees fall open, revealing the deep rose of her pussy, I see the sheen of wetness on her delicate skin. Her chest rises and falls as I look my fill. I love the way her tits move, and I remember how it felt to wake up with one of them in my hand in Vegas. We've wasted so much time since then not doing this. I see no reason to wait a second more, so I sink to my knees in the kitchen and take a long, wet lick along my wife's seam.

She groans, deep and guttural, and I know she's unaware of doing it. One of her hands flails around, finding the top of my head and patting my hair as I take another lick. I vary my pressure, ignoring the hard floor against my knees as I study Emerson's micro-movements in response to what I'm doing. She likes the broad, flat strokes of my tongue better than the flicks. She jerks closer to the edge of the counter when I suck on her clit, finding the hidden pearl as I press my palm into her thigh.

I pause briefly to look up and admire her, all messy and disheveled. "What's happening?" She tries to sit up. "Is it over?" The look on her face is pure torture, and I love that I am already getting her so worked up.

"No, Salty. It hasn't even started yet." I slide a finger inside her, and she remains propped up on her forearms, watching. "You like that? You like watching me fuck you with my hand?" I withdraw my finger, and her breath catches, so I slide it back in alongside a second digit. Her eyes practically roll up into her head. I'm tempted to drag this out all night, but I remember that this is new to her, so I decide to have mercy and let her come sooner than later. Keeping my fingers inside her, I crook them up as I suck on her clit again. When her thighs clap together over my ears, I know this is what she needs to get off. I'm in heaven with creamy skin alongside my face and her taste on my tongue. My dick throbs in my pants but I don't want to stop any of my work to palm myself for relief. I can wait. It'll be worth it.

Emerson screams and shrieks and pulses around my fingers, and I pull my mouth from her body but leave my fingers in place while she thrashes around. This gorgeous woman is here for me. Not because of my family, not because she heard of me online, but because she met me and wanted me for myself. And I'm going to make it worth her while, coaxing as much pleasure from her as I can. Once she's whimpering and still, I stand up and suck on my fingers, licking the flavor from my hand as her eyes open and her hands fall to the counter.

"Damn, you're gorgeous when you come." A lazy smile turns up the corners of her lips, but she seems too wrecked to move. I'm glad I could bring her that release. My dick jumps in my pants and I give it a pat. He'll have to wait until I'm in the shower later since Emerson didn't seem on board with going any further today.

I lean over her body to kiss her, feeling her nipples against my chest, drawing a deep moan from my throat.

"Gunnar," she whispers, hands in my hair. "I'm a virgin."

CHAPTER 13
EMERSON

"What's that?" He rests his chin on my sternum and gazes at me, looking a little drunk as if he just orgasmed instead of me.

I glance around, looking for my clothes. Gunnar notices and grabs the jersey he was wearing. He bunches it up in his hands and approaches me, and I realize he's going to put it on. Me.

"I never had sex before," I tell him before I silently hold up my arms, and he dresses me in his shirt, stooping to grab my underwear from his kitchen floor. He then holds them open, and I instinctively place a hand on his shoulder and step in.

He stands in front of me, running his hands down my cheeks, staring into my eyes. "Emerson, I'm so honored you let me do that for you."

I blink, confused. I wasn't expecting him to laugh at me exactly, but he seems … grateful? That I "let" him get me off? "I want to do more things with you, I think," I stutter. "But I don't know what to do, and you're so good at it, and I need you to be patient when I mess up."

"Salty." He presses my hand to his chest, where I can feel his pulse thundering. "You are my best fantasy. I am hard every time I so much as think of you. Whatever you want to do or not do, I'm going to enjoy the hell out of it."

I snort, overwhelmed, worried I'll cry again if I think too hard about him being this nice. "Thank you, I guess." I lean forward and kiss him on the cheek, and he pats my hand. He stretches, revealing a glorious bit of abdomen, and asks if I want to watch anything on TV.

Before I can respond, he's hopped over the back of the couch and arranged himself, flicking on the giant device. I walk around to sit beside him, unsure where to place myself on the couch. Do we snuggle now? Should I go to my room and give him an out? There's no actual protocol for post-oral activity with my accidental husband.

I'm rescued from these thoughts by the strong band of Gunnar's arm snaking behind me and pulling me close, and I really have no choice but to lean against his side, my bare thigh pressed against the cotton of his sweatpants. "What do you want to watch?" He keeps his eyes on the screen as he clicks around.

I shrug, and he turns to face me. I clear my throat and explain, "I never get to watch TV. If I'm home with downtime, I'm supposed to practice and prepare for my auditions..."

"Hm." Gunnar frowns. "I've had plenty of try-outs, and I still manage to rot my brain with *The Walking Dead*." He must notice my expression because he chuckles. "We can skip the zombies, though, and start with *Yellowstone* if you want? It's about cowboys."

"Cowboys?"

Gunnar nods, and the television erupts with sweeping

landscapes, running horses, and beautiful actors in tight jeans.

I relax against him even as the plot gets a little intense. I can't keep track of who is who, but someone has stolen a horse, and someone else stole some cows. Through it all, Gunnar keeps his arm around my shoulders and toys with my hair. It seems unconscious, like he's not aware he's winding the curls through his fingers, but it feels mesmerizing. I might fall asleep like this.

"Are you comfortable?" His voice cuts through the pink haze.

"You know, I really, really am. Like…so comfortable."

He squeezes me and says, "Good. Me, too. We should implement a house rule where we are always dressed just like this." He turns his head and ogles my body, or what he can see of it squeezed against him and hiding beneath his shirt. I like the fact that it's a bit big for me. I like being near someone larger than me, who seems to not just tolerate my body but enjoy it. He said as much while he was rocking my world.

I squirm a bit on the couch. "That might get a little cold in the winter, don't you think?"

"Nah. Stag men are always hot. We have furnaces inside." He pats his stomach, which is a solid slab of muscle. He doesn't have a six-pack that I can see. It's more of a stone tablet of abs behind a wall of smooth skin. I see a light trail of fuzz beneath his navel and blush, wondering what lurks below the waist of those pants. His chest rumbles as he begins to talk again. "Are you cold? Shit, I don't even have a blanket on the couch. I told you I suck at living alone. I'm going to order a blanket. You need anything from Costco?"

He has his phone in his hand before the cowboys on the television finish brushing their horses.

"No," I tell him. And then I remember something. "Did you say you have a bucket of lube on your fridge?"

He nods. "Safe and Satisfied. That was a huge thing with my parents. Is there something you want to add to the basket?" He looks up from the app, thumb poised to apparently scour for sex toys or something. I shake my head.

Once Gunnar finishes his phone order, he throws his phone on the coffee table between his feet, and I curl up closer, utterly surrounded by his scent and … the smell of what we did together earlier. It's all very heady and warm, especially with the sensation of Gunnar's fingers running through my hair.

For some reason, it feels wrong to nod off, so I focus on his body to keep myself alert. I see a tendril of ink near the collar of his shirt, and I tug it down a little, seeing a tattoo. He meets my eye, and I peek down the shirt. Gunnar laughs and pulls his shirt off. "Have a look."

I see that he has a deer leaping over some foliage tattooed on one pectoral and a bunch of different designs wrapped around the opposite shoulder and upper arm. Is that called a sleeve?

I reach out a finger to touch the antlers of the deer tattoo. Gunnar glances down. "Ah. That's the family ink. A stag leaping over laurel." He smiles. "We all have it somewhere. Dad and his brothers all got it to honor our grandma Laurel." He pats the tattoo affectionately. "Mom has a similar one. And my aunts. It's a rite of passage now, to go get the family tattoo when we turn eighteen."

I connect my finger to his, tracing the outline of the ink,

enjoying the way goosebumps spring up on his chest as I lightly touch his skin. "That's so nice that you all do that together. I could never get a tattoo."

He presses my hand flat against his body. "Why the hell not?" When I look up into his eyes, he's frowning, confused.

I laugh, a humorless sound. "Performers simply do not mar their bodies that way, Gunnar." I can hear it again in my voice, the snap reaction to the oppression I came here to escape. "My father would catch fire with rage."

"Well," Gunnar pats my hand and drops his back to his lap. "He's not here, and I've got a guy. I can get you an appointment tomorrow if you want. Ink you up real good."

When I laugh again, it's a much lighter sound. "I think I'm okay."

He nudges me with his shoulder. "We can get PROPERTY OF GUNNAR blasted on your butt cheeks."

"You are obsessed." I'm soaring now, warm and comfortable and so, so relaxed.

"Damn right I am, Salty." And he reaches down to pat the body part in question. "It's a fine ass. In fact, we shouldn't do a thing to it. Get your tat somewhere else."

If I don't stop laughing, I will get the hiccups, so I tell him I'll think about which design I want to get and where. To my surprise, I actually consider it. What would it be like to have the design of my choosing permanently marked on my body? I recall the website I saw for that cello band. With their brightly dyed hair and edgy outfits, they seemed like they'd welcome a performer with a tattoo without hesitation. Would ink on my arm distract me as I play? Would I prefer a design that's more private?

I must drift off to sleep with these thoughts because when I next open my eyes, it's morning, and I'm snugly tucked in my bed, a glass of water beside me on the nightstand and a note scrawled on a napkin:

SLEEP TIGHT, SALTY

CHAPTER 14
GUNNAR

Emerson is still sacked out when I stop home after morning skate, so I don't get a chance to talk logistics with her until lunchtime. Tonight's the home opener, and she'll be there cheering with my family. The idea makes me happier than I have any business being, and this morning, I was on fire on the ice, blocking shots like it's my job.

If this keeps up, it will stay my job.

After our team meal, I look around the locker room, realizing I'm going to have to phone my fake wife within earshot of my brothers and, worse, the team.

Sighing, I shoot her a message before I head in for my massage, and mercifully, she calls when I'm alone in the therapy room. "Hey." I keep my voice low and realize I sound really husky. Whatever.

"Hello. Thank you so much for…Well, I assume you carried me to bed. I hope I didn't injure your spine."

There's a genuine note of concern in her voice that I try to bat away immediately because Emerson is the perfect amount of wife. "You were utterly conked out, Salty. And I barely noticed lifting you." I hear a small, appreciative sound, and I sit up, swinging my legs around so they're dangling off the padded table. "I was checking in with you about the game tonight." Emerson is going to sit by the ice with my family for tonight's game against Detroit. I offered to set her up in the fancy box with the other PAWs, but Dad convinced her she'd enjoy herself more by the glass.

"I'm ready whenever," she says. I hear the sink turn on and a clatter of dishes, and I frown. I don't like the idea of her doing my dishes. I guess some of them could be hers, but I really wish she'd leave them for me to take care of. I like taking care of her, darn it.

I scratch my chin. "Mom wondered if you were in for the double header or just wanting to go for the Fury. She's planning to pick you up."

"Oh, I can take the bus. I don't want her to go out of her way to—"

"Emerson. You're my wife. You're not taking the bus." I grip the padded table so hard I might have torn through the vinyl.

"Gunnar. You're my husband. I have taken public transportation my entire life." There's an aggressive-sounding clunk, and I hope she didn't crack my giant breakfast bowl.

I pinch the bridge of my nose and explain, "Em. Apart from the fact that I don't want you riding an unfamiliar bus in a strange city, you have to think about what the press would do about Gunnar Stag's wife showing up at the arena on a bus."

She sighs. "I hadn't considered that."

"Right. So…Mom can either grab you—"

"What do you mean double header? Are you playing twice?"

"Nah. There's a women's exhibition game first. Trying to drum up support for the new pro league. You don't have to go…"

She inhales audibly. "I want to! I want to see the women play. I didn't know there was a league for women."

I scratch my head and jump off the table when I hear the therapist and the next guy arriving for their rub down. "Yeah, it's pretty cool. Okay, so Mom will grab you in…" I look at the clock. "Oh, shit. Like a half hour. Is that still good?"

"Yep. I'm ready. I've got my G-Stag shirt and my face paint, and I am ready to go."

Now I'm dying to see her all dolled up with black and gold face paint. I send a quick note to Mom to bring a spare hat and blanket for Emerson, just in case, and head off for my warm-up, excited to show off for my wife.

I wish I could see my family during the women's game, but we're sequestered for film and nutrition, so I have to rely on Dad sending me periodic updates on the women's team goalie—competent, Uncle Tim's mood—pissy, and my gorgeous wife—enthusiastic AF. I chuckle at a picture of Emerson pressed against the glass, roaring. I can just make out the gold G STAG letters on the back of her black jersey, which she has on over a turtleneck.

Seeing her amped up like that for hockey, when I know she grew up totally repressed in a house that literally only cared about music…is really doing it for me. Coach glares at me as I slide my phone into my pocket, but I'm feeling more focused and ready than I was a week ago, and this intriguing woman is a big part of that.

For the first time since I joined this league, I'm burning to go when we finally line up in the tunnel to take the ice. I don't usually do a lap—my gear makes that awkward as hell, and I prefer to get set up in the net. But my girl is sitting by the blue line, and I have to flash her a grin. My girl...I need to stop thinking that way. She's not mine to keep. But she's sure as hell mine right now. I wave at her and damn near do a back flip when she blows me a kiss.

The camera crew notices, too, because I catch sight of her up on the jumbo screen, dancing and waving and having the time of her life. A small nugget of worry digs into my gut that this will wind up in a tabloid somewhere and make things even more difficult for her with her parents. Still, all of that is overshadowed by the cavemanesque delight I take in having her sitting with my family, cheering for me. Sure, she's excited to see my brothers, too, I guess. But it's me she's locked eyes with as I stretch.

When the puck drops to start the game, I tap into the same focus as always. The world disappears apart from the puck, the hips and skates of the opposing team, and the sounds of blades and sticks on ice.

I'm blocking shots like a solid wall, not noticing the time passing, barely feeling the sweat I know is soaking my hair and running down my legs inside my heavy pads. I'm acting without thinking, but now that's expected of me.

When the lights begin to flash and the foghorn blares, the crowd starts screaming "STAG, STAG," and I know one of my brothers scored. Fuck yeah.

Eyes back on the puck, I send every ounce of my energy into deflecting shots. Our defense is outstanding, making my job easy today. I almost can't believe it when the game ends and I haven't let a single biscuit by.

"Hot damn, Gunny!" Alder pounds me on the back as Tucker approaches on the other side to pull my helmet off and kiss me on the cheek. Camera flashes explode in the stands as we celebrate together. This is what it was all for, I realize. My family is here watching me celebrate the game we all love. The fans are happy with a win that our city will celebrate.

The three of us make our way to the boards, and Coach is, while not exactly smiling, decidedly not angry. He grunts and nods, a massive seal of approval from him, I'm learning. The team manager tugs at her collar and shouts over the din. "Media! G Stag, Cappy, Dallas. Go!" My brothers make eyes at me and give me a few more shoves as I hobble back to the locker room in my skates.

I'm a little surprised to see a blonde woman in hockey gear leaning against the wall. "Are you from the women's team?" I take my place beside her, waiting for the reporters to kick into high gear.

She rolls her eyes. "Yes. I'm dying for a shower."

My face contorts in horror. "They made you wait this whole time?"

She shrugs. "I might have taken my gear off and put it back on after the third period of your game."

"Shit. Sorry. That's really rude." I extend a hand toward her. "Gunnar."

She smiles, returning my shake. "Ashley."

And then we're swarmed. The Fury PR lady, I think her name is Kehlani, whispers that we're doing a joint interview with the women's team goalie since we both had shutouts, and that's part of the deal in cross-promoting with their league.

"Okay, but did they really have to make her wait two hours to shower?"

Before Kehlani can answer me, the reporters are in our faces with cameras, asking the typical boring questions about how it feels to get a win. I'm all ready to talk about my shutout, proud of how I worked toward that this week, when the reporter pulls a U-turn and asks Ashley about her husband. "He's a starter for Boston, isn't that correct?"

Ashley's brow furrows, and she nods.

"And you play for Pittsburgh. How is that working for you two? The distance?"

Clearly uncomfortable talking about her relationship, Ashley says, "It's definitely my goal to be signed with a team in the same city as my husband, but for now, we work it out. We're both very dedicated to our teams. It's a fantastic opportunity to—"

"Are you able to support your husband at any of his games?" The reporter interrupted her to ask about her husband when Ashley is here to talk about her own game. This blows.

I reach for the mic, seeing red. "Hey, I notice none of you have asked me about my spouse yet. But that's okay because I'm happy to tell you how awesome she is. She's a musician."

There's silence as the reporters seem to absorb my nonsequetor. Ashley's chest shakes a bit with silent laughter, so I turn to her. "Do you listen to music before games? I personally don't because it's too hard to deal with those little earbuds once I start gearing up."

Ashley nods, pursing her lips. "I do, actually. I have a playlist. Helps me focus. But I do okay with the earbuds."

"You must have been pretty focused today. You had a shutout." I grin and hold up my hand for a high five.

She returns the gesture. "Yeah, you, too, Gunnar."

The reporters don't seem to know what to make of the

goalies taking over the interview, and they all sort of drift away. Eventually, Kehlani claps her hands and dismisses us.

"Hey," Ashley says before she waddles out of the locker room on her skates. "Thanks for that."

"Yeah. Any time. You'll have to send me your playlist."

She beams. "I'll do that." She gives me a salute and slips out the doors just in time for half the guys on the team to strip naked.

CHAPTER 15
EMERSON

I AM HAVING SO MUCH FUN—ACTUAL FUN, COMPLETE WITH jumping and yelling. Is this how other people just go about their lives this way? I can hardly believe how much I like this family.

Gunnar's parents wait with me until he and the twins emerge from the locker room, dressed in jeans and T-shirts for our planned outing to what Gunnar calls a "chill bar" in a neighborhood called The Strip District. The name gives me pause, but my husband assures me it's not called that for clubs and pole dancing, but rather the steel strip mills that used to operate there.

The door to the locker room opens, and a mass of giant men emerges, many stopping to shake hands with Gunnar's dad on their way past us. I'm no stranger to having a famous father in my same professional field. But when I see Gunnar approaching, he doesn't look anxious or upset by his father greeting his teammates the way I would with mine.

Gunnar barely seems to notice at all, in fact. Gunnar locks his blue gaze on me, and … I feel a pinch and tingle between my legs. I spent the day today doing research, hoping to get some time alone with him later to repay all the pleasure he gave me. A muscle in Gunnar's jaw moves as he swallows, and he walks right up to me, past his parents, dipping to kiss me on the cheek. "You look beautiful," he whispers, his smile illuminating his entire face.

I bring a hand to my cheek, where I can still feel remnants of the black and gold face paint I recently washed off in the bathroom. I took off the turtleneck and borrowed ski cap, so I'm just wearing a jersey and jeans with my hair in pigtails. A casual look I would never, ever have considered in public before today. It's one thing with this group, at the arena, where pretty much everyone is dressed this way. I'm still anxious about going out into the bar with Gunnar, where I know there will be fans with phones and photos.

But I forget to worry about all that when he tucks me against his side and his brothers announce that Ty and Juniper will drop us at the brewery the team rented out tonight for players, friends, and family. Ty grins as he steers us toward the ancient minivan, and Gunnar rolls his eyes. "Dad, you couldn't bring Mom's car?"

Gunnar opens the sliding door for me as Ty points out, "If I had, you and your brothers wouldn't all fit, now would you? Emerson, you sit behind Juniper. The twins will do just fine in the third row."

Alder and Tucker groan, climbing up and over the seats and cramming themselves in the back of the vehicle. I bite my lip and stamp down the guilt I feel at taking a spacious captain's chair while the massive hockey players are so cramped. But the trio of brothers is soon joking with their parents about the game, so I try to accept that they'd tell me if it was actually a problem.

Juniper turns in her seat. "Are you sure you're ready for this?"

Ty brings the van to a halt and puts on his blinker, in line to drop us at the door. "Ready for what?"

Alder laughs. "Oh, three hundred or so rabid hockey fans. Hey! Tuck, did you say the women's teams are here, too?"

Tucker grunts an affirmative sound, and my eyes widen. "I didn't realize it would be so big."

Gunnar leaps out of the van on the driver's side and rushes around, offering me a hand. "It will feel small, I promise. We'll set you up in the corner near the nice PAWs."

"Paws?"

Tucker claps a massive hand on my shoulder, meeting my eye. "Partners and Wives. They'll take care of you, even if you did shun them up in the box tonight."

"Shun?" Had I already made a faux pas in this arrangement? I thought I did everything Gunnar said I should.

I feel mildly better when he elbows his brother in the ribs, making Tucker double over. "Don't be like that, fucker." He turns to me. "Em, nobody cares that you sat with my family. I promise they'll love you. Let's go inside."

Our entrée into the building is so vastly different from a post-concert cocktail party that I really am not sure how to walk, where to look, or what to do with any of my body parts. Ever since the tabloid article yesterday and messages from my parents, I've been on edge, despite the dopamine injection from orgasms with Gunnar. I'm glad when he laces his fingers among mine, clasping my hand and tugging me forward. His voice booms above the rock music on the sound system as he says, "Cam, Essence, meet my wife, Emerson."

A white man and a Black woman wearing Fury jerseys turn and smile at me, and the man throws his hands in the air. "Finally! We see her! Essence, she's more beautiful in person, isn't she?"

Essence nods. "We read all this crap online and saw all those out of context photos." I'm not even sure what images she might be referring to, but I wince all the same. Whatever it was will just add fuel to my parents' outrage. What will it look like if they start responding? Retaliating?

I remind myself that I'm secure right now. I have what I need.

I smile at my new companions. "Well, it's nice to meet you, too. I'm new to all of this." I gesture around.

Cam nods and looks at Gunnar. "Well don't be a douchebag, Gun. Get her a beer. We're having the autumn ale." Cam smiles at me. "I promise it's good. Come sit!"

He and Essence gesture toward a wooden bench at one of the long tables in the back of the pub, which is spacious, featuring two long bars, hustling wait staff carrying trays of food, and throngs of excited people in Fury gear, as well as a large group of women in hockey jerseys, whom I assume are the women I watched play earlier. I smile and accept the drink Gunnar offers, reminding myself to muster the nerve to approach them and tell them how much I enjoyed watching their game.

Cam is dating a Fury player named Banksy, while Essence is married to the captain, who seems to be named Cappy. Beyond us, only a few of the current players have partners. Essence rolls her eyes and explains, "The team is in a rebuilding phase, which means the guys are young … which means they're a bunch of promiscuous sex fiends."

As she talks, I notice some of the players getting friendly with women approaching them for autographs. Judging by the body language I'm seeing, the sex fiends will be happy.

Cam leans his elbows on the table and asks, "So do you know anything about hockey?"

I shake my head. "Today, I learned what a puck is." I laugh nervously at first, then more freely when Essence and Cam chuckle knowingly.

Cam tells me he started dating Banksy about a year ago. "Banksy is my first athlete," Cam says, clutching his chest. "But I'm still a theatre brat at heart."

My eyebrows shoot up. "I'm a symphony brat. So, sort of similar."

Cam leans forward again. "Have you ever been in the pit for any cool shows?"

I shake my head. I'm about to begrudgingly explain my former life, awkwardly, when Gunnar taps me on the shoulder. "Hey, Salty. Come take a photo with me."

"A photo?"

He nods. "Yeah, they have one of those selfie stations." He points to the wall, where a group of female fans jump and clap as the Fury players hold glittery props and party hats for photos. My stomach drops at the thought of all that attention, but Gunnar squeezes my hand, and his brothers appear at my other side.

"Welcome to the family," Tucker says. "We travel in packs."

Cam and Essence give me a thumbs up, before returning to their beers when I start to move amidst my herd of Stag men.

I chuckle softly as a group of young women starts tugging at Tucker, pleading with him for photos. Some of the fans hold printed copies of the selfie booth images, hold up markers, and ask for autographs. It's much more intense than the reception lines I'm accustomed to after a performance. And, frankly, the goal here seems more about physical connection than financial gain. However, as I look around at the excitement, I decide it's all the more genuine. These athletes are performers as well, and why shouldn't their fans feel thrilled to spend time with them after their game.

I'm probably reading too much into a sour look from one of the women as I make my way closer to my husband, who appears to have been swept up in the crowd of admirers. Alder remains at my side and lifts an arm protectively to usher me closer to the selfie station, but I'm soon jostled out of the way by a group of guys and women who are begging to get pictures with all three Stags.

The next thing I know, Alder is getting cozy with a guy in a tank top while Tucker has a woman under each arm.

I try to push my way back to my table, to the relative comfort of Cam and Essence, at least, when I notice Gunnar hugging one of the female hockey players. He seems genuinely happy to see her, and I had wanted to talk to the women's team anyway, so I take a deep breath, square my shoulders, and walk toward them through the crowd.

"Gunnar." I place my hand on his upper arm and then, noticing once again how firm his muscles are, give his arm a squeeze. "Who's this?"

"Hey! Ashley, this is my wife, Emerson."

Ashley beams. "Your husband is so rad. He totally saved my post-match interview from being a misogynistic shit show."

My brows shoot toward the exposed beams in the ceiling. "How did he do that?"

She rolls her eyes and waves a hand. "It's too loud here to go into. You'll find it online, I'm sure. But you've got a good one. Emerson, was it?"

I nod. "Yeah. Thank you. I really enjoyed watching your game. I didn't even know there was a pro women's league."

Ashley is shoved from behind by a wave of people, and she reaches for my arm, steadying herself. She guides me toward the bar, where there's more room. "Woo, that's getting intense over there. Anyway, yeah. The women's league is new. Supposedly, there will be some expansion teams next year."

I look around for Gunnar, wondering where he went. I spot him trying to disentangle himself from an older woman who is attempting to kiss him on the cheek, bright lipstick leaving a smear on his face. "Man," Ashley says. "They really do treat them like meat samples, don't they?"

I roll my lips between my teeth. "Is this normal? You know this is all pretty new for me."

"Oh, yeah. I notice it when I go out with my husband. I've been at this my entire life, and I still hate it. So, you're absolutely right on track."

I'm not sure how I feel about this "chill bar" experience being the norm for the rest of my life with Gunnar, but I remind myself that we are only in this for six months. Six months to get himself situated with his starting position and endorsement deals, and then I will pretend to break his heart and return to…a future still to be determined, I guess.

Gunnar must have shaken off the aggressive fan because, when he makes his way to Ashley and me at the bar, he's alone, his eyes boring into mine. His arm snakes around my waist, and I feel instantly better, more secure. I listen politely as he and Ashley talk about goalie things. At least, I think that's what they're discussing with all this stomach chat and mental preparation references. It's definitely related to hockey gameplay.

I reach for my neck idly, where in another life I'd wear pearls, but finding none, I remember Gunnar's offer from the other day, and I remember my research on that offer… alone in bed with my phone. The thought of it thrills me, which shocked me at first. I saw a few videos of the type of pearly necklace Gunnar joked about. My face heats at the memory of the fantasy my mind created about doing that with Gunnar.

As I remember our time together in the kitchen, I know that anything we do together naked will bring surprise and pleasure unlike anything else. Like he said, we're in this for half a year. I realize that sex could add yet another layer of complication to our situation, but is the potential for explosive pleasure worth that risk? I can already sense that he'd make every encounter enjoyable for me. I just worry I might not be able to return the favor.

I absentmindedly run my fingers along his forearm, trying to decide, until Gunnar takes a deep breath.

"Ashley, it was awesome meeting you. Hit me up anytime. But I gotta get out of here."

She nods and gives him a salute, melting back into the crowd on her way toward the other female players. Gunnar abruptly spins me to face him. "Salty. You're killing me."

My brow furrows. "What? What did I do?"

He shakes his head. "Tracing those damn fingers all up and down my arm, standing there. Looking hot as fuck in my jersey. And you're making sex faces. We have to go home."

"Sex faces? Home?"

He leans in, his lips brushing against my ear. "If I don't get you home immediately, I'm going to fuck you right here on this bar, and I don't think you're ready for that."

I blink, pressing my legs together at the thought of his naughty words. "Oh."

"Damn right, oh," he says, striding toward the door and tugging me behind him. Outside, he raises his arm in the air toward the line of cabs outside the brewery, and before I can blink, I'm skidding across the back seat with a very large, very turned-on hockey player pressed against my side.

CHAPTER 16
GUNNAR

"Holy shit, you're Gunnar Stag from the Fury." Our driver is turned around, staring instead of racing up Smallman Street toward my apartment.

I nod, draping an arm around my wife and grabbing a handful of boob when she presses against my side. "I am. And I'd love you to drive me home. Please." I flash him a grin, and he keeps shaking his head.

"I never got a pro athlete as a fare before. This is so great."

I drag a hand through my hair, anxious about being stuck here for another hour making small talk, but Emerson steps in to save the situation. She leans forward. "Do you want to give me your phone and I'll take a quick pic of you two? Really quick before we get moving?"

The guy beams, pulling out his phone and fiddling around in his hurry to unlock the screen. I scoot forward and give a thumbs up as Emerson leans back to get us both in the shot. "Perfect," she says, handing the driver his phone.

"My kids are never gonna believe this. I should call them right now and tell them Gunnar Stag is in my cab."

I'm about to leap out and just walk home, but Emerson smiles. "We would be so grateful if you could get us home. Gunnar is exhausted from his win tonight."

The guys' brows shoot up. "Yeah! Of course. At your service." And he gives her a wink before zipping out onto the street.

I kiss her on the cheek, relieved that she soothed the fan without pissing anyone off. Usually, I'm good with this sort of thing, but college hockey fans aren't nearly as wild as the pros, and I'm in a pretty thick fog of pheromones here with Emerson in a Stag jersey, making sex faces.

The driver continues to talk about hockey, rattling off stats about our team and our upcoming opponents. I could be back here making out, but I know it's in my best interest to listen. I try to grunt at the appropriate times, and thankfully, the ride is pretty quick. Before I know it, my wife is tugging me out of the back seat and looking like she's about to pay the driver.

I growl at her as I reach for my wallet and hand the guy a hefty tip before slamming the door and scooping Emerson into my arms. "You know I love opening the door for you, Salty. Were you about to pay that cab driver yourself?"

She grins. "Is that so terrible? You've been paying for everything, and I have hardly left the apartment."

I roll my eyes and pull her close, kissing the top of her head. "The whole reason you're here is because of me. And it feels better if I'm being good to you."

"Mmm." She hums and looks up at me, then bites her lip. I'm not drunk on alcohol, but the rush of hormones flooding through me makes it feel like I'm halfway blitzed on Emerson alone. "You want to be good to me?" She traces shapes on my chest with her fingertip. I nod, palms on her ass now. She has the most perfect ass and I love how it feels cupped in my hands. Her voice is low, barely perceptible. "I looked up the pearl necklace…"

I'm instantly hard, panting at the thought of doing something so dirty, so primal with this woman. "You did?"

She nods. "I think you should give me one."

I cannot explain how we get to the apartment. I don't know which of us unlocks the door or slams it shut behind us. All I know is we are splayed across Emerson's bed because it's the closest one to the door, and I'm nestled between her thighs with my tongue in her hot little mouth. My dick is so hard I'm worried it will rip through both our pairs of pants. Actually, that wouldn't be a bad thing because then it would be touching her silky skin.

"Salty, you really want to do that? Do you want me to come all over that pretty neck?" I lick along her throat to illustrate my intentions.

"God, Gunnar, yes. Please. I want to see you come." Her legs wrap around me, insistent, pulling me against her center where she's hot and soft. I can't believe she wants me to be a jeweler for her.

"I gotta get you there first, Salty. I'm going to eat that perfect pussy again until you're screaming my name. But then you have to tell me if you want to drop to your knees on the floor for me or if you want me to fuck your tits until I make a mess of you in this bed."

The words falling out of my mouth are obscene, but it seems to drive Emerson wild because the more I talk, the more she moans and rubs herself against the hard ridge in my pants. Her hands move to my waist, fumbling with snaps and zippers. I pull back from her just enough to rip her clothes off, and I grunt appreciatively when I see her naked.

"You are so incredible, Emerson. God, look at you. Just look at you." I drag my palms down her nipples, and she moans. I nip at the skin of her rounded belly, nudge at her thighs with my nose.

"I want you naked, Gunnar. I want to feel you." Her eyes flash in the dim light as she grabs at my shirt and tugs. I let her pull it off over my head before I dive back down to get my mouth on hers. She rips open my pants and grabs my cock while biting my lip and I realize I've somehow unlocked a wild, horny layer of Emerson's personality.

"Salty," I whisper against her mouth. "You're desperate for it."

She nods. "You make me this way. I keep thinking about you doing those stretches on the ice."

I laugh. "You like when I stretch?" I pinch her nipple as she sucks in a breath.

I decide to get down to business and kick my way out of my pants, pushing her thighs wide enough for me to lick and suck and slide a finger inside until Emerson is pulsing and shrieking. In minutes, her hands drop to my hair and she holds me against her center while I fuck her with one hand and lap at her clit. She comes loud and long, and I lap up every single moan. "Mmm," I whisper. "You *did* need it bad, Salty."

Her hands flop to the mattress as I kneel above her, giving my dick a tug while I try to decide what comes next. "Are you ready for this? Because we don't have to do anything you don't want."

Emerson's gaze snaps to mine. "We're doing it."

My mouth hooks to the side in a grin, and I look around her room. I spy a row of cosmetics on the dresser. "Go get your lotion," I command, and I almost come in my hand when she obeys, climbing out of bed to grab a small container and scurrying back while she opens it.

I lick my lips and continue casually pumping my wood. She scoops out a handful of lotion, fragrant and fresh smelling. "Can I rub it on you?" She looks up at me hopefully, as if I might deny her this request.

"God, yes." I rock back onto my heels as she sits in front of me, both hands working the lotion into my shaft. She circles my tip with her thumb, concentrating on her work with the same expression I've seen her wear when she's making music. "So good," I sputter. "You feel so perfect."

"Really?" She smiles then, enjoying the praise, and I know this won't take much longer.

"Lie back," I growl. My voice is low. "Press your boobs together."

Emerson's face is indescribable as she settles on her pillow, hair a mess, peachy nipples hard and pointed at the ceiling. Her palms cup the sides of her boobs and press, leaving a heavenly channel for me to slide inside. When I do, we both groan. I might die from the pleasure of seeing my dick disappear in between her boobs, but when I thrust forward and the tip pokes out, she sticks out her tongue and laps at the crown of my cock.

I pull back, shocked into ecstasy, and my hips start rocking without my knowledge until I'm driving into her, grunting. We both moan when she licks the tip of me again, and I dig my hands into the headboard as I come, giving her the hot ropes of my release like she asked for.

Emerson screams my name and pants with each splash hitting her skin.

My breath is ragged and hopeless, and I am wrecked when I collapse beside her. But she moans in pleasure, writhing around on the bed. One hand traces the mess I left on her chest, and the other dips between her legs. "Gunnar, that was so, so sexy. Holy cow, I need…I need…"

"Ugh." I see that my wife needs me again, needs to come after seeing me lose myself like that. I join my hand to hers at the top of her thighs. She rubs at her clit while I slide a finger inside her and together, we pull her over the edge.

I should get up and get her a washcloth, clean her up, get her clean again. But I pass the fuck out with her chanting my name as she drifts off to sleep, marked by our shared desire.

CHAPTER 17
EMERSON

I wake up feeling warm and relaxed, but as I move to sit up I'm a little sticky. Nothing a shower won't fix.

The bed is rumpled beside me, and I realize that Gunnar slept here with me. I'm not sure what to make of the rush I feel at that awareness. So, I grab his shirt from the floor, pulling it over my sticky body, and pad to the kitchen, where he's scribbling a note at the counter. He has a bag draped over one arm and a giant bottle of ... something ... in his hand.

"Oh, hey, Salty." His grin shines bright in the gray light of early morning. It must be very early. He slides the note to me, which reads

You're beautiful, wife

I smile and point at his bottle. "What's with the sludge?"

He glances at the liquid and frowns. "The trainer says

I'm supposed to drink this before my first workout. They feed us during film before we get out on the ice." His brows shoot up. "What's on your plate today?"

I tug on the shirt, feeling a little chilly, but I don't miss the way his gaze lingers on my legs at the hem or the heat in his eyes at the sight of me in his shirt. Gunnar likes identifying me as *his.* I realize I like it, too. I like him, this unexpected husband of mine. Things feel right with him, like I'm able to really be myself. If I could just figure out who that is…

I sigh and tell him, "I think I'm going to look into that school I saw. For kids into music."

"Awesome. Let me know if I can help." He glances at his watch. "I gotta run, but I'll be back this afternoon." And he steps toward me, kissing my cheek as if it's a regular part of our routine. Gunnar's out the door before I pull my hand from my face, wondering why it feels so real if we're just here playing pretend.

It's not typical to feel so at home with a man I just met, right? And yet, Gunnar and his family have been so welcoming. They make it impossible not to fold into their fabric. It seems hardly a lie that we fell for each other immediately…from my end, anyway.

I finally shower, reluctantly putting Gunnar's shirt in the wash and considering pulling a dirty one from the pile just to smell him all day. "That's gross, Emerson," I chide myself, wondering if I can think of some excuse to sniff him later without it being weird. Is he open to more regular physical connection? Maybe he's just leaning all the way in while this lasts…tightening the ruse as he gets closer to signing the contracts he wants?

I sit at the counter with his laptop and consider my

options. I would absolutely love to join the String Fury music group, but I don't even know if they're auditioning for new members. Such a niche organization likely receives a thousand hopeful musicians contacting them every day.

I decide that the Scale Up Music Academy is a more approachable first step for me in establishing a purpose here in Pittsburgh. According to the website, students from under-resourced backgrounds can attend music classes at no cost, receiving instruments and even concert clothes for free. The school emphasizes many different styles of music, ranging from European classical to African drumming to Punjabi. My spine tingles with excitement at the idea of working in that sort of environment, helping kids discover the power of music and allowing them to explore the sounds and rhythms that feel right to them.

No one at Scale Up appears to be forcing children to play one particular type of instrument. Based on the photos online, there's a balance of genders in all of the ensembles. I'm ready to float away as I click the button to apply to work with the organization ... until I'm faced with the reality that I have no job experience and nothing to put on a resume for the application.

I don't have a resume. I've never been employed. I've performed in various places, but I lack experience in providing instruction. I don't even know how to be a receptionist.

My eyes dry out from a lack of blinking as I confront the crushing fear of having to go back home. My parents believe they provided me with everything money could buy, and perhaps that's true. But it came at a cost.

Here I am, unable to flourish without them.

I can't work in a music school for underprivileged youth.

I can't work anywhere. I don't know how.

There's another tab on the website for volunteers with the program, but I realize I can't do that either. Volunteering with children apparently requires background checks and clearance paperwork. That seems just as out of reach to me as a job offer.

I slam the laptop closed and walk down the hall to the music/trophy room, smiling at the memory of Gunnar nicknaming it "the McTrophy room." I pause in the doorway, noticing that Gunnar has been organizing his things here. A bookshelf now occupies one wall, the kind with many cubbies. Each cubby displays his hockey awards, and while several boxes remain on the floor, they are neatly stacked.

The chair in the middle of the room and my cello are the focal points now. He's carved out space for me, no questions asked. This man is as wealthy as my father, I assume, yet he doesn't use his money as a weapon. Instead, he's eager to make me comfortable, however I define that.

On the verge of tears, I hear a buzz from the kitchen. My phone dances across the counter with incoming messages. I risk a glance at the screen, fearing more tabloid or family drama, but see it's from Gunnar.

> Hospital gala Friday night. Can you make it? Would love to have you at my side, Salty.

He even sent a little emoji of a salt shaker. I stare at my phone, realizing that there is something I can contribute here in this city. I can be arm candy at a society event. I can help a wealthy man schmooze at a fundraiser. That's what I was born to do, right? I type a response.

> You bet.

I include an emoji of a dancing woman. I spend the rest of the day grooming myself, shaving, polishing, and moisturizing, so I'll be ready to play my part.

CHAPTER 18
GUNNAR

"How's married life, Gun-town?" Our first line center flicks a puck at me.

I kick it out of the way without having to look at it. "Better than your wrist shot, Rogers." It's not even a lie. Rogers has a hell of a wrist shot, but living with Emerson is incredible.

She's always really happy to see me when I get home from practice, whether I watch at the door while she finishes playing or if she's in the kitchen making us a snack when I arrive.

We cuddle on the couch and watch TV until I fall asleep. Then she wakes me up, and I always want to tug her into my bed, or sneak into hers, so I can spoon her all night. But I guess there's time for that. We've got months left on this bargain.

Grentley is back on the ice today, but coach has me in the net while he works on the starting line. Grentley is not happy about it. I don't blame the guy, but what does he want me to do? I'm playing great, and I know that's because I've got an amazing home life. Brian kept pushing me to appeal to screaming fans, when it turns out I just needed an incredible woman loving me to really reach the next level.

Robert snaps another puck my way, and I have to stretch a bit, but I block it with my glove, dropping it behind the net for Alder to scoop up as he makes an arc along the boards. From my perspective, practice is going great.

I don't say this to the guys, but I'm sure it's Emerson's influence. She keeps me in a great mood, allowing me to train better. When I train better, I perform better. I'm even starting to feel like I've earned the right to be here. Okay, maybe I got signed in college because of the name on my back. Perhaps I was able to come up early after my brother's injury because of the same name. But our starter is healthy, and coach still picked me today.

I block another set of shots until I hear the whistle announcing the end of practice. I'm totally caught off guard when Grentley shoves me against the wall in the tunnel to the locker room. "What the hell, man?" Regaining my balance, I shove back at him. Not hard. Because it's the same team.

He grunts and stomps ahead of me, turning a corner without explanation.

"Big baby," I mutter, yanking off my gear and thanking the equipment manager, who hauls it away. I have a rotation I can barely explain for my leg pads and neck guard, but this guy always hands me the right shit and it hardly even stinks.

I try not to think about Grentley's tantrum, which is difficult because he's over in the showers oozing a black cloud of negative energy. The rest of the guys don't seem to pick up on it. Morale is high as we head into our first real matchup this weekend. I've got the gala Friday night and then a home game against Buffalo on Saturday. That means I'll get to see Emerson in that dress … and then Emerson in my jersey. Everything's coming up Gunnar.

Brian sends a thousand messages while I'm in the shower, reminding me about the gala and who I have to suck up to at the hospital. I immediately think *Emerson will help me with all that* and then realize I've already come to rely on her for that stuff already.

I know it's technically pretend, that we're playing house. We're also having explosive sex that's both dirty and more intimate than I'm going to admit out loud.

I finish up in the locker room and whistle my way to the car, driving home to my wife…who I find staring out the window in a semi-dark apartment. "Hey." I drop my bag and approach her from behind, startling her. "What's up?"

She turns, smiling, and stretches up to kiss my cheek. "Hey yourself." She walks to the counter and grabs an apple, beginning to slice it like I didn't just find her staring into the Allegheny River.

Emerson slides me half the apple, and I place my hand on top of hers. "What's up? Something's different about you." When she shakes her head, I raise a brow at her. "You were just staring out the window in the dark, and now you're slicing up fruit like a robot. Talk to me, Salty."

I bite into the apple, and she slumps forward, shaking her head. "I don't know what I was thinking. I can't work with the music program. I can't work anywhere."

I slide onto the stool across from her. "What do you mean? Why not?"

"I have no work experience. You can't gain experience without experience. Apparently."

"Hmm." I pop another apple slice into my mouth and nudge the cutting board toward Emerson, who hasn't had any yet. "I know what you mean. This is actually my first job, too." She huffs. I laugh. "Isn't that wild? First job? Pro hockey goalie."

"My first job was supposed to be with the symphony. So, I guess it's not wild to me."

We munch on fruit until the apple is finished. I scratch my neck, deep in thought. "You've played gigs before, though. Don't those count as jobs?"

"You've played games before, too."

"Fair. I got endorsements in college, though. Small ones." I hold up my thumb and forefinger close together, recalling the low four-figure checks from video games and, once, a soup cracker deal. I pat her hand. "You'll figure this out, Emerson, because you're tough and smart. But let me know if I can do anything, okay?"

She shrugs, still looking down, but she agrees to cuddle with me on the couch while watching *Yellowstone,* so the evening still ends on a good note.

Emerson's mood is low the next few days, but by Friday she seems to be all business. The plan is for me to rush home after practice, jump into my tux, and she'll arrange for a car to get us to the gala. I have half a mind to walk since it's only a few blocks up the hill, but my bride will be in heels, and that hardly seems fair.

We haven't talked about anything substantial for the rest of this week, and we haven't hooked up again either. It's as if we're really married now, stuck in the rut of routine. But a man can dream about his curvy wife in her sexy dress, right?

By the time I get myself situated on Friday, she's dressed and smelling amazing. A scarf is draped around her shoulders, and her hair shines, cascading down her back in loose waves. I can't focus on my tie after seeing her. It feels like the dress has become sexier since I last saw her try it on. Or perhaps she has just grown more beautiful the more I get to know her.

"Salty. Damn." I swallow.

A gorgeous pink flush creeps up her cheeks, but she says, "You look nice, too, husband."

"You're not going to give me a nickname? I worked so hard on yours."

Emerson snorts. "I'm not really a nickname person. You might be the only person I know who uses one."

"Ah, babe. You can do it." I finally get the tie sorted and dust off my shoulders, giving a little spin as she assesses me with a nod and a smile.

She sticks her tongue out. "What about Smalls? Because you're so big…"

I wink at her. "I remember telling you to always remind me of that."

We talk about nicknames as we wait for the elevator, as I open her car door, and as we pull up to the event. We get ushered into a new therapy suite in the hospital for kids with injuries. I learn that they have the most up-to-date rehab equipment for pediatric patients.

"Mr. and Mrs. Stag? Right this way." A staffer greets us at the door. Emerson seems ready to just brush inside, but I pause.

"My wife is Ms. Saltzer."

The young woman's brows shoot up. "My apologies, sir. I will make a note of that for next time." She hurries off, muttering into her headset.

Emerson frowns. "You didn't have to do that."

"I did. They had your name wrong. What if there were place cards?"

She rolls her eyes. "Gunnar. Your whole job here is to make people feel comfortable." She gestures around the room. "These are the wealthy donors. You are the face of the organization. They can call me Mrs. Stag."

"Well, I would like them to call you Ms. Saltzer."

She's about to snap back at me, but someone else approaches us at high speed. Another staff member, by the looks of it. "Mr. Stag, we were hoping we could get some photographs with you and some of the patients before things get rolling in here, if that's okay?"

I nod. "Of course." This is why I'm here. Kids and puppies. Or just the kids, I guess.

Tugging on Emerson's hand, I prepare to follow the staffer alongside her, but the guy appears uncomfortable. He winces. "Actually … um…"

Emerson smiles and pats my arm. "Gunny, honey, they only want you." I grimace, and she pats harder. "I will be just fine out here. Go meet your fans."

And then I'm swept away to some patient rooms, where a few adorable kids tell me about their broken bones and torn ligaments while I sign hockey sticks and jerseys, smiling for the camera. This stuff is easy. I don't even have to fake any facial expressions with kids. They make the best fans. It's only when they get older and try to invade my privacy that I get twitchy around them.

"What's up, little dude?" I approach a hospital bed where a kid with both legs in casts. He looks tired.

"Hi," he says, in a flat voice.

"What's up? You don't like hockey?" I squat down so we're eye level.

121

He shrugs. "Not like I can play anytime soon."

I whistle and gesture to his legs. "Yeah, that looks pretty uncomfortable. But you'll snap back for next season, right?"

He turns away and stares out his window. "If I can make the team next season."

"Hey," I lean in closer to whisper. "I've been sidelined for a full season before. In high school. Groin pull."

He turns back, his eyes wide. "Yeah?"

I nod. "Seriously. I promise they'll remember you next year." The kid brightens after that, and I sign a jersey for him, taking a selfie with him before I'm dragged back to the gala. If this is what Brian wants me to do to establish myself as a household name, I'm golden. I love this shit.

The gala room is much fuller now, filled with people in their finest black and whites sipping wine. My gaze locks onto Emerson as she chats with the team owner, and I'm drawn to her like she's pulling me across fresh ice. She's so at home right now, talking and gesturing, a smile brightening her face. Except it's not the same smile I'm used to.

I realize she's performing right now. My heart sinks at the thought that I've placed her in a position her father often does, to schmooze with wealthy people for an agenda. Sure, it's a hospital fundraiser and an objectively good agenda. But I don't like knowing that I'm just another man in her life asking her to smile and look pretty for the rich folks.

I'm about to reach for her, kiss her on the cheek, when the director of the hospital shouts, "Ah! Gunnar Stag! The man of the hour."

I turn to face him, smiling with my own performance expression. Brian prepped me for this. "Flaherty. Great event. Thank you for letting me be a part of it." We shake hands very enthusiastically. "Have you met my wife, Emerson?"

Flaherty's expression must be genuine as he smiles at her. "I had the pleasure just moments ago. My heartfelt congratulations. I understand the happy event occurred right after our agreement! I don't mind if I do assume that our partnership inspired your nuptials."

Emerson's laughter is a tinkle, like little bells in the stuffy space. "That must have been it. Gunnar is genuinely excited about interacting with all the children."

"I'm sure he is, darling. Have you met Bradford Rollings from the Kent Endowments?"

I lose sight of the puck with all the names tossed at me. As the night goes on, I shake hands with various fancy people while keeping one arm around Emerson's shoulders, impressed at the way she keeps the conversation light and focuses away from herself. She remembers everyone's names and facts about them. I feel like a stranger in a strange land, but I smile and thank them for their support whenever Emerson squeezes my hand.

I'm surprised to realize that a few hours have passed, and after several speeches and rounds of applause, we're all dismissed into the night. One thing is clear to me: I owe my wife big time for her help this evening, and even more because giving me this support put her in an uncomfortable position.

CHAPTER 19
EMERSON

We pass through the hospital's sliding doors into the crisp autumn night, deciding to walk home. Gunnar has taken off his tux jacket, loosened his bowtie, and rolled up the cuffs of his dress shirt, looking sinfully good with the black coat slung over one shoulder. He whistles as he places a hand on my lower back and steers me down the hill toward Butler Street.

I squeeze his arm. "That was kind of fun. Did you get to meet any of the kids?"

He nods and makes a contented sound. "The kids are great. I had no idea what to do with myself for the rest of it." He gives my bottom a squeeze and then doesn't move his hand away. "I was really glad you were there to talk me through it all."

Warmth spreads in my chest at his remark. "Well, you know, I can rub elbows with the best of 'em."

Gunnar makes a low sound and then pauses at the corner. "I feel like I've put you in an awkward position, asking you to do that when you came here to get away from that kind of thing."

My mouth drops because he's right. And yet tonight felt different. I never once felt pressured to say anything specific or promise anything beyond a whirlwind romance with the man of the hour. "Gunnar, I…I had fun tonight. I enjoyed talking you up."

"Yeah?" His crooked smile is adorable.

"Yes." I nod. "Truly."

Gunnar presses a kiss to my forehead. "You hungry, Salty? I could eat an entire cow." He stabs the button for the crosswalk signal and glances at me, questioning.

"I could eat."

And then he grins, his white teeth glinting under the streetlights. Does he really have to be so handsome? I could maintain boundaries and keep things chill if he didn't look so good. It's all well and good to have dirty sex, but if I'm going to disappear in a few months, I can't be falling for this man emotionally. I clear my throat. "Your coach mentioned something about a shoe deal? That you're going to shoot a commercial?"

He nods and gestures for me to turn left. We approach a bar, and he holds the door open for me. "After you, Salts. Maybe I should call you Shaker. Salt shaker. You want a burger?"

I laugh at his train of thought. "A burger sounds awesome." I move to grab a seat at the bar, but he hesitates, and I remember that he's famous. The bar is crowded, yet there's a small table near the window, so I slide into a seat, and he surprises me by sitting next to me rather than across from me. "You're feeling cozy!"

Another grin. "Can't stand to be far from you, Shakes. Oooh, milkshake! If we're going to wreck my meal plan, I might as well do it in style, right?"

The bar has one of those QR code ordering systems, so

Gunnar pulls out his phone and orders us fries, burgers, and chocolate shakes. He turns his phone upside down on the table and turns to face me in his chair. "The shoe deal is really new, and the commercial is for the milk campaign. I was going to talk to you about that. I'll be staying in New York a few extra days after our game there to shoot the ad."

I take a moment to digest the fact that he's traveling to New York. "I hadn't stopped to think that you'd be going there. To the city."

Gunnar nods. "Yeah. You know I have a lot of road trips coming up, actually." He licks his lips and furrows his brow. "Brian thinks it could be really beneficial if you come with me. Make it seem like you're visiting your family while you're in town."

My eyes fly wide as the bottom drops out of my stomach. I actually press a hand to my belly to calm my roiling guts at the thought of seeing my parents in person right now. "My family?"

Gunnar nods. "Yeah. Obviously, I told him I had to run that past you, especially since part of our story is how you need to maintain privacy to get away from your family…"

A server arrives with our food, and Gunnar keeps his head down, hoping to avoid being noticed, I think. I smile, thank them, and take a big gulp of my shake. "I can't really think of a good excuse not to go see your game. It's not like I have anything going on here in Pittsburgh." I smash a fry into my shake and eat it in one bite.

"First, it's freaking weird to dip a French fry into a milkshake, wife. Gross." I stick my tongue out at him and do it again while he shakes his head. "Second, I thought you were going to help those kids who don't have music lessons at their schools. What happened?"

I cram another fry into my mouth and sigh. "I can't even volunteer there because I don't have the necessary legal clearances or whatever they're called. I need some sort of background check, and I have no idea where to start. They don't teach you this kind of thing in frou-frou music college."

I slouch down in my chair and pick up the burger, relishing the salty, savory flavor. The tiny appetizers on trays at the fundraiser were lovely, but this food truly hits the spot, and I'm so grateful Gunnar suggested stopping here. I moan in delight, and his brows shoot up.

He clears his throat and adjusts his posture. "Salty, I want to get back to your disgusting fry habits in a minute. But I can probably help with the clearances. We have to have them to work at kid clinics and charity stuff like tonight. Brian has people who handle that for me. I'll just have him handle it for you."

I shake my head. "Oh no, I don't want to bother him with that. He's out there trying to secure your image or what—"

Gunnar holds up his phone, showing me a text exchange in which he asked Brian to get me clearances, and Brian responded with

> Consider it done.

"Now." Gunnar puts the phone in his pocket this time. "Why on earth are you contaminating your milkshake with fried potatoes?"

Helping me and getting other people to help me, is just like breathing for him. He doesn't even seem to think twice about the effort involved in getting me what I need. I'm uncertain what to make of it, so I roll with his decision to switch topics to fries. "You clearly haven't tried it, or you wouldn't be dissing it." I dip another fry and hold it toward him. He presses his lips together and shakes his head. "Come on, husband. You know you want to." I dab at his lip, catching a small drop of milkshake on the corner of his mouth, causing me to think about licking it off.

From the flash in Gunnar's eyes, I sense he's thinking the same thing, but it passes quickly as he opens his lips, accepts the fry, and considers it. He chews a few times and shrugs. "Not bad."

I bump him with my shoulder. "Is that all you have to say? After giving me so much grief about it? I think you owe me a proper apology."

The air in the room goes silent, or at least it feels that way when Gunnar meets my eyes. His blue gaze turns dark, his jaw set. A muscle or tendon or something twitches in his neck. "How would you like me to make things up to you, wife?"

I bring a hand to my mouth, wondering what to say and how to respond. My heart pounds in my chest at the thought of him doing something sexier than I ever dared to imagine, and at the thought of me loving every second.

Both our phones vibrate, interrupting the moment. I frown, not wanting to check mine in the pocket of my dress, but Gunnar slides his hand into his. I half hope the messages are from Brian, informing us know there's a problem with the clearances, but Gunnar growls when looking at his screen.

I peer over his broad shoulder to catch a headline alert from an online tabloid.

Maestro Makes Musicians Miserable

Renowned conductor Charles Saltzer of the New York Symphony is facing mounting allegations of creating a hostile work environment for female musicians in the orchestra. Multiple sources report that Saltzer routinely dismissed qualified female candidates, made demanding comments about their performance and capabilities, and enforced archaic policies specifically targeting women.

The allegations come on the heels of his daughter, Emerson Saltzer — Juilliard graduate and accomplished violinist — abruptly leaving the classical music scene. Maestro Saltzer claimed that the young musician was addressing mental health concerns.

This publication wonders if a respite from the senior Saltzer was in itself an improvement to the younger Saltzer's wellbeing.

This is a developing story.

I stare at the article, reeling. I've been holding my breath, waiting for something awful to come out in the news about *me*. I've always been led to believe I was the problem- the diva, the difficult musician basically making my parents' lives harder.

This article is junk journalism, to be sure. But it's not about me.

I don't know how to feel about other people giving voice to these suspicions I've had that my father is a jerk. That my father is the problem. I start sweating and breathing heavily as my reality is shattered.

"Hey." Gunnar's hand is gentle on my thigh, squeezing. "You want to go home?"

I nod rapidly and take a final gulp of my milkshake. He sets a bunch of cash on the table, wraps his tux jacket around my shoulders, and ushers me out the door toward our apartment.

CHAPTER 20
EMERSON

I'm numb back at the apartment, as if I can't figure out my next moves beyond kicking off my heels.

I keep repeating the word "hostile" in my mind, jarred by seeing someone else, albeit an anonymous editorial reporter, refer to my father that way. Hostile is exactly right. My entire life has been a hostile environment. I had never encountered that phrase before seeing it on Gunnar's phone.

I always thought I was so fortunate, getting to make music (even if it wasn't the music I wanted) and to live in such wealth. I never lacked anything.

Although, that is not true. As my unexpected hero ushers me into my room and gently unzips my dress, his hands gentle on my back as he slides the gown down my shoulders, I realize I've never experienced this kind of caring physical touch.

"You are so important to me," he says, palms skating along my skin. "I can't believe I asked you to come to New York and act gooey for me with all this crap going on in your life."

I lean into his touch and shake my head. "It didn't feel gross. Not when it was for you." My lashes are wet, and my chest tightens. "I know you aren't expecting it…that you appreciate me."

I stand in my fancy underthings, staring at myself in the mirror above my dresser, still motionless as Gunnar hangs up the dress and grabs my G STAG jersey from where it's folded at the foot of my bed. I let him slide that over my head and melt into him when he pulls me into his arms, kissing the top of my head. "I definitely appreciate you. What do you need, Salty? I'm here."

He rubs my back soothingly. Instead of feeling better, I think of the contrast of my father's harsh words when he'd come home to hear me practicing a difficult passage—or Dad's sneer when I was seated below second chair after an audition. Gunnar's voice is low and strong near my ear as he says, "You're an amazing person, Emerson. You make beautiful music and always know what to say to make people feel special."

I pull back and look up into his handsome face. He smiles down at me from his considerable height.

"Will you stay with me tonight? In here?"

Gunnar nods, smiling even wider than before. "Of course I will."

As I stumble back toward my bed, he kicks off his tuxedo pieces, leaving them in a heap on the floor—a stark contrast to how he took such care with my things. He climbs into bed with me, wearing only a pair of tight, black underwear. At first, I'm nervous about sleeping beside him like this, but he's so warm, and his arms around me feel so safe and strong. It's like hugging a hot water bottle.

I know things are supposed to be pretend with him... but this feels awfully real.

I watch my hand rise and fall on his chest as he breathes, just lying there silently, holding me.

"They're going to come looking for me," I tell him.

"Who is?" His fingers feel nice stroking my hair.

I shrug, as much as I'm able while cocooned in his comforting nest. "The press. My family. They'll want me to help with damage control."

"Hey." Gunnar lifts my chin to meet his gaze in the darkness. I can make out enough of his expression to know that he's serious. "I will do whatever it takes to keep you safe and comfortable, Emerson Saltzer. My family can help us with anything legal, and my teammates can help create a physical fucking wall around you if that's what you need. Got it?"

I nod, blinking back tears. "Thank you," I whisper. And then I fall asleep to the reassuring rhythm of his heartbeat.

I worried things would be awkward when I woke up tangled in Gunnar's limbs, like that first morning in Vegas. But I open my eyes to his sleepy gaze, blinking and studying me as I ease into wakefulness. "Don't you have practice?" Gunnar usually leaves the house before it's light outside. Granted, I have no idea what time it is currently or whether it's daytime. My room doesn't have a window.

He smiles. "It's early still."

"Mmm. It's nice having you here. Thank you for staying with me."

Gunnar's eyes widen. "Are you kidding? I feel fantastic. You're like a soft, silky bathrobe. And you smell incredible."

I huff out a laugh. "Okay."

"I'm serious." He inhales a long sniff of the top of my head. "Some sort of magic potion. What is that smell, anyway?"

I purse my lips, trying to think. "Well, I use a lavender chamomile shampoo …"

"I want to bathe in it. You have to wear a hat all day, and then let me put the hat in my locker. Oh my god, that's it." He sits up. "That's going to be my 'thing' this season. Salty Hats."

"Your thing?" I sit up, stretching my spine, fingering the sleeve of the jersey.

Gunnar grins as he stoops to pick up his crumpled tux. His back is long, lined, and muscular, and his backside is thick, round, and at eye level…"You know hockey guys are superstitious, right? You have to know that."

I shake my head, drunk on thoughts of his butt. "You know I've spent my whole life in an orchestra pit, right?"

He laughs. "Well. Salty. I need a ritual and now that I'm getting some ice time, I *really* need a ritual. It'll keep me focused."

"Do your brothers do these things? Locker hats?" I stand and stretch, walking to my dresser for a pair of pants I can tug on.

Gunnar walks down the hall toward the bathroom, yelling over his shoulder, "You'll have to ask them. They're pretty gross. You might not want to hear the answer."

I smile, appreciating how lighthearted and fun he can be while also taking his sport and career seriously. Gunnar has shared that he feels he didn't earn his spot on this team…that he got there based on his father's reputation. Those sorts of thoughts sometimes flitted through my mind, especially during my time at Juilliard, but I also know that I'm an excellent musician. In some ways, I think we excel in our fields because of our parents—these sorts of proclivities tend to be inherited. However, Gunnar and I have both worked extremely hard to refine our craft.

I'm vaguely aware of him getting ready for practice as I comb my hair, wash my face, and attempt to carry on with the normal parts of my day, even though I can tell I'm too upset to make music today. My phone rings, and I answer it out of habit, stumbling when I hear my brother's voice.

"Emerson, we need to talk."

Edwin is stern and cold like always. An attorney, he's used to people doing as he asks.

Frustrated, I snap, "Nice to hear from you, too, Ed. Thank you for the lovely card you sent after I got married."

"I most certainly did not send a card acknowledging that farce."

I roll my eyes at his inability to comprehend sarcasm. "What do you want?"

"You know that I'm calling about the news article. Mom is apoplectic."

I walk into the kitchen and yank open the fridge, unsure of what I'm searching for. "Mom is always apoplectic. Why is this different?" I realize I feel bold today, that I'm standing up for myself with my brother. My time with Gunnar has already changed me, and I let the lightness of that realization lift me up a bit more.

His voice is a hiss. "There's going to be an *inquiry*. From the *board*."

Locating a bottle of cranberry juice, I grab it and pour myself a glass, not bothering to mop up the red splash on the counter. "Well, I imagine they will discover some things, Ed."

He growls. "Emerson, do you really want our family dragged through the press over some angry outbursts? Conductors are perfectionists. It's pretty universal."

As I listen to him defend my father and talk about all the ways men will be boys, I realize quite clearly how immersed I've been in that mindset, too. Running away on that train feels less and less like a mistake with every day that I spend with the Stag family. I truly escaped something awful.

"Edwin." I interrupt my brother, possibly for the first time in his life. His sharp intake of breath indicates his surprise at my doing so. "That behavior is universal among mean men who can't accept that the world is changing. If women feel uncomfortable in the symphony, we should listen to them and act differently."

He starts to sputter something about orchestras sounding just fine without women, and I see red. "Do you really think you're helping to convince me to defend Dad? Are you seriously dismissing women's contributions to professional symphonies?" My brother is just like my parents, viewing me as a pawn or something put on this earth to uplift my father and his precious reputation. I can't listen to him another second. I snap, "Find someone else to listen to your crap."

I hang up on my brother, slam my phone down on the counter, and chug the rest of the juice, wiping my mouth with the back of my wrist. I turn to see Gunnar leaning against the hallway wall, watching me with a smile on his face.

"Nice take down, Salty." He winks. "Grab your coat. I'm buying you breakfast."

CHAPTER 21
GUNNAR

AFTER BREAKFAST, I DROP EMERSON BACK AT THE APARTMENT, where she says she's going to work out her frustrations on a minor fugue. Whatever that means. I secretly wish I could leave a recording device open or a webcam or something so I can listen in between sessions today at the rink. Her music is incredible on a good day, and I'm dying to hear what she cranks out when she's deep in her feels.

But recording my wife without her knowledge sounds like something her parents would do, and that's gross. Anyway, I have meetings today with Brian.

I park and flash my badge at the building entrance, slapping a high five to the door guy and whistling as I head to the locker room, where Grentley growls at me, and my brothers are busy swapping socks.

Alder pokes his head out of his cubby and snaps his fingers at me. "Hey."

I raise one brow at him. "Hey?"

"You seeing Brian today? He wants to know if Tucker and I will do a gum commercial." He reaches into his sleeve to apply deodorant and then takes off his shirt. His warm-up rituals are seriously odd, and I'm saying that as someone who just asked his wife for a hat to sniff.

"You and Tuck will be amazing in a gum commercial, bro. Why wouldn't you say yes?" I start arranging my things so I can put them on, setting my gloves and mask to one side and hanging up my chest protector. Grentley continues to give me the stink eye as if he's not doing the same shit.

Alder groans. "It just feels like one more thing. I don't know."

I check my pants, neck guard, and knee pads, and set them to the other side. Alder is already halfway dressed while I'm still pulling shit from the bag that the equipment manager wheeled in front of my locker. My brother watches as I step into my goalie jock. He points at it. "Speaking of blocking cock..." I glare at him, and he laughs. "You're bringing Emerson to Stagsgiving, right?"

I yank on my knee pads. "Of course I'm bringing my wife to our Thanksgiving." *I need to ask my wife about Thanksgiving...*I step into my pants, and Alder starts lacing his Bauers.

He scratches his neck as I start strapping on the leg pads. He scrunches up his face and says, "I want to see if Adam will come. With me. To thanksgiving."

I pause midway through pulling on my right leg pad. "You're getting serious with that guy from the bar? That's cool. I still need to meet him."

Alder shrugs. "Yeah. Thanksgiving might be like trial by fire."

Coach hollers that we have two minutes to get on the ice. I hurry up tying my chest pads to my pants. Alder hesitates, clearly wanting to get out to practice but also not finished discussing it. "Hey," I tell him. "We could go out —just me, Em, and you two—ease into it?"

He taps his fingers on his helmet and nods before jamming it on his head. "Yeah. Thanks, man." And he's gone, leaving me wrestling with my jersey on my own.

Morning practice is pretty great apart from Grentley snorting and stomping around. I appreciate that my brother felt he could share with me about his relationship. I like that I was able to comfort Emerson when she was upset last night. Although she grew up in the limelight, she's clearly new to this kind of press and people getting up in her business in an invasive way. I sometimes forget how much those articles can sting. Frankly, I think there's more truth to that article than not. I wonder if Emerson has someone to talk to about the shit her parents put her through.

As I hurry back out of my gear to meet Brian, I try to remind myself to check on that later.

Brian is seated in the cafeteria, where all the guys are being served their specific post-ice time and pre-cardio nutrition. Mine is a protein shake that won't make me poop. My pants are literally laced to my chest pads. I can't risk that sort of digestion.

Brian smiles, sipping his own shake. "G Stag! Baby! Come sit."

I do, taking a swig of my gloopy drink.

Brian slides a folder over to me. "Look at these images of you with the kids, G Stag. Golden. Perfection. I love it. The milk people love it. The mommy bloggers love it."

"Thanks?"

He nods. "We need to get you out there a bit more,

though. You doing the fan fest in New York? Don't bother answering. You're doing it. I'm thinking it's crucial to have your lady there with you, too. The PAWs can get matching shirts, right? Who would order them shirts?" Brian scribbles something on the folder as I keep sipping my drink. A lot of the time, it feels like I don't really need to be present for these agent meetings.

But I also feel a creeping sense of unease as Brian rattles on and on about how much the press is going to love seeing Emerson beside me at the fan event and how she will look in a Stag jersey. It feels manipulative, as if I'm some other dude like her father, just wanting her to play a part. I don't want her to play a part with me…I want her to enjoy being with me. That realization makes me really happy…not at all what I expected. "What if she doesn't want to come to New York?" I fiddle with my empty glass. "Things aren't good between her and her family."

Brian nods. "I saw the article. However, we need her to be there. We can arrange for her to stay in the hotel where the team is staying in…try to avoid mentioning her family. Has she received any media coaching? Let me send someone to your place."

I wince at the thought of that. "I need to ask her before you send someone, Bri. Come on."

He sighs audibly and finishes his drink, crumpling the paper cup. "Fine. Talk to her. Text me. Get your brothers to say yes to the gum thing! They're being weird, G Stag. Why are your brothers being weird?"

I laugh. "I don't know, man. Don't I have enough going on without bringing them into it? Maybe they're just weird."

He cackles. "You sound like your old man." He slaps the folder shut and stands, holding a hand for me to shake.

"Text me about the media coaching, kid. And don't think I forgot about the puppies."

I also stand, heading toward the door and our off-ice cardio session. "Hey, I wanted to thank you for the help with Emerson's clearances. Did those come through?"

Brian doesn't look up from his phone but waves a hand. "Necessary, G Stag. She'll be with you and the kids, right? For the photos? She's all set with that. Give me ten minutes, and I'll get her a pdf of everything but the FBI fingerprints. She's on her own for that, unfortunately."

"Unfortunately? I hope you don't have fixers faking FBI fingerprints."

Brian pivots toward the exit as I continue straight down the hall. He hollers over his shoulder, "I have fixers for almost everything, Gunnar. Almost."

CHAPTER 22
EMERSON

Gunnar insists on driving me to the Scale Up Academy building before he heads to his pre-game activities at the arena. When the courier delivered my clearances yesterday, I almost cried in relief and immediately clicked to volunteer with the music classes. The director texted me within minutes saying they need all the help they can get.

So, here I am, missing a Fury home game, but Gunnar assures me that nobody can possibly attend every match. "We sometimes play four times a week, Salty. You need your you-time." He pulls up in front of the building and leans over to kiss my cheek.

It seems like an innocent enough gesture, but my nerve endings didn't get the memo that he was just being supportive. No, my body starts screaming at me to grab his collar and cram my tongue in his mouth.

I'm breathing heavily when I say, "Good luck tonight. Is it okay to say good luck to a goalie?"

He nods. "Yeah. What about you? Do I tell you to break a bone or is good luck okay?"

I laugh. "We don't do good luck. You can tell me to

have a good show, except I'm not performing. So maybe it's okay to wish me luck?"

He runs his fingers through my hair, and I shiver at his touch. "All good things, Salty. I'll see you later tonight."

As he drives away with a beep, I wave and head inside. My phone vibrates, and I check it, thinking it'll be something cute from Gunnar. But it's just more upsetting crap from my mom.

> I raised you to support this family, not destroy it, Emerson.

> That hockey player punk has turned you against your duty.

I power down my phone and walk up the stairs, where I'm greeted by a frazzled Latina woman in bright red glasses. "Hi, I'm Lucia." She looks behind me. "Did you bring your young person?"

I grin. "I'm Emerson. I emailed about volunteering." I shrug. "I'm here to work."

Lucia moans and dramatically slumps in her chair. "Oh, thank god. We are so shorthanded." She peers through the door, where I hear a lot of blurts and thwapping sounds. "Can you help Omar with the tuning? Just... anything you can do will help."

I nod and walk into the main room, where a line of kids fiddles with various instruments that are sorely in need of tuning. The rows of chairs are filled with adults trying to read or occupy younger siblings. The noise is deafening. Making my way to the front of the line, where a young dark-skinned man is wrestling with a tiny cello, I tell him, "Hi. I'm Emerson. How can I help with tuning?"

He stares at me. "You're the string player, right?" He

pushes the neck of the cello in my direction. "I can't move these tuning pegs."

I take a seat on the edge of the stage and gesture for the instrument. I study the instrument and nod at the young owner, a red-headed girl wearing overalls. What I wouldn't have paid to be allowed to wear overalls and play the cello at her age! "Hi," I tell her. "I'm Emerson. What's your name?"

"Erin."

"Well!" I pat the stage next to me. "Let me show you some tricks for this." I pull a bar of soap from my bag and show Erin how to dab just a little bit on the pegs to lubricate them.

We get Erin's cello tuned, and I look up to see that Omar has all the brass instruments in his line and has funneled the strings toward me. Within a few minutes, or what feels like just a few minutes, we get the kids all tuned and divided into smaller practice rooms with their instructors.

Omar says it's fine—in fact, really helpful—if I pop in and out of the different string lessons to help kids with their body positioning while the teacher works with the groups.

I've never enjoyed anything more, and that includes all the fantastic experiences I've had with Gunnar as well as performing at the Sydney Opera House. These kids are bright and eager to learn about music. It holds a sense of mystery and discovery for them, and their enthusiasm makes the lesson all that much more exciting.

I was crammed into classical style lessons starting in preschool, but these kids are experiencing music for the first time as elementary-aged kids. I love that I'm a small part of their instruction, of stoking that fire they feel for the music.

The turnover between sessions is rapid enough that I don't get a chance to chat with Omar or Lucia, but I'm more prepared this time and feel confident greeting families and guiding kids toward a line to have their instruments tuned. The second session is comprised of older kids who have a little bit of experience, and I enjoy it just as much because these kids understand the effort involved in making music, yet they still choose to be here.

I'm sweating, exhausted, and overjoyed when the final family clears out. Lucia grabs at her lower back, and Omar whistles. "Great job today, team. Emerson, you good?"

I smile and sit cross-legged on the stage. "I'm great. When do you need help next?"

Omar laughs. "Um, every day? All day? Seriously. How much time you got?"

I explain that I'm currently not employed. "Music is incredibly important to me. I have both the time and enthusiasm. I want to help!"

Lucia starts gathering her things, shaking her head. "Well, I don't know what we did to deserve you, but we'll take it, Emerson. See you tomorrow afternoon?"

The academy is an out-of-school organization, so their hours are naturally in the evenings. I'm a little wary of cutting into time I could be spending with Gunnar, but I don't have the time to unpack that urge. "You bet," I tell Lucia. "Can't wait." And it's true.

I walk outside, determined to figure out which bus to catch toward my apartment. I looked up the routes, and I'm pretty sure I can catch an 88 every few minutes at this time of day. But I'm thwarted by a pleasant honk and a woman leaning out of her car window, hollering my name.

It's Gunnar's mom.

"Juniper?" I walk toward her black SUV.

She beams. "Gunny said you might need a ride home. I wasn't sure when you'd be finished. Hop in!"

My mouth drops open, but I walk around to the passenger side and climb aboard. The vehicle smells like food…and my mouth waters immediately. Juniper smiles. "You hungry? I thought maybe we could eat some pho and chat." My stomach gurgles loudly, and we both laugh. "That settles it, then."

She starts to drive. I tap my hands on the bag on my lap. "You're not going to the Fury game? Aren't all three of the guys playing?"

"Meh. They have plenty of games. I let go of the guilt about missing their games a long time ago. We'll watch it on the TV, of course." She smiles.

I nod. "Of course."

Juniper asks me how things went at the music school, and I talk her ear off during the drive, telling her about all the joy they showed in their instruments. "And the music selection is so fun! They're playing a song about hot dogs."

Juniper parks on the street and grabs a takeout bag from the back seat. "Nothing like a song about food to put everyone in a great mood."

Up in the apartment, I can tell that she's used to moving about this space, but she hesitates midway through setting up the game on the giant TV. "I'm sorry," she says. "This is your house, and I'm barging in as if I own the place."

I shake my head. "Not at all. I don't know how that thing works anyway."

She laughs and gets back to work, pulling up the game,

while I grab us bowls and silverware. I appreciate how Juniper sets up the food on the coffee table, where we can be comfortable eating on the couch. This family is so casual yet so intimate. It's easy to feel good around them. It makes me realize how much of my life I've spent feeling bad.

"Do you eat meat? I wasn't sure, so I got one chicken and one veggie. We can split them…"

"Mmm," I interject. "I eat everything." We work together, scooping the soup into two giant bowls, along with the rice noodles, bean sprouts, basil, and lime. Juniper dumps hot sauce into her soup and offers me a packet, but I scrunch up my nose and shake my head. "Okay, so I don't eat *everything*."

We're quiet as we watch Gunnar, Alder, and Tucker being announced as starters, and Juniper eats a big bite of her soup before saying, "I was so sorry to hear about the article. Gunnar's Uncle Tim asked me to share that he is ready to help, legally, however you might need. You know, he's already Gunnar's lawyer, so he's pretty looped in."

I furrow my brow. "Legally? What would that mean?"

She leans back against the couch and takes a slurp of broth. Swallowing, she says, "Things might get dicey if your family wants to retaliate against whoever wrote the article." My expression must reveal my unease about the whole situation because Juniper squeezes my leg. "I want you to know we've fought this kind of crap before, and our family is here for you, okay?"

My throat is dry, and I take a sip of my soup, not sure what to respond to her offer. "I don't even know what I would do. I've just been hoping it will all die down." I haven't answered my parents' calls, and the longer I avoid speaking to them, the more I realize that it's a healthy choice for me right now. I have space here to discover what I like, to eat when I'm hungry, and to wear clothes that make me feel good.

I know I stumbled into this as a drunken mistake, but every day in Pittsburgh feels more and more like I have finally found my real life—the one I'm meant to live.

Juniper sighs. "Honey, I don't think it will blow over so easily. I haven't met your father, but I've met men like him."

I frown. "Meaning?"

She looks at me, quite serious. "He's wealthy and powerful, and someone is threatening that. When people feel threatened, they act in their own interests and often don't consider the people they harm in their wake."

Her words ring in the air as Gunnar blocks a shot on the ice, and the announcer screams his name. We hear a roar from the crowd that continues as the camera zooms in on him. He's smiling—beaming, really. I know in my gut that my father will attempt to wipe that expression from his face.

CHAPTER 23
GUNNAR

COACH IS FOCUSING EXTRA ATTENTION ON THE GOALIES during practice this week as we prepare to hit the road to New York. I played pretty well in our home games, but Grentley is back to 100% and I can tell he's pushing to reclaim his starting spot back.

The pressure to get out there and stay out there is worse than actually playing in the game. Once I'm on the ice, I'm focused and confident about what I can do. This horse shit with him shoulder-checking me in the locker room and glaring all the time? It drives me bananas.

Emerson actually gave me a hat to put in my locker that she wore for hours, so I give that a big huff before I get dressed.

Across the bench, Grentley stares at me creepily while lacing his pants to his chest protector. I'm partly impressed that he can tie all that without looking and partly pissed off that he's pulling these kinds of juvenile intimidation tactics on his teammate. I think about Emerson, growing up in a house with a bully of a father, and how she pulled up the courage to hop on a train and escape. Grentley and his bad attitude are nothing compared to that.

I sniff the hat again, and with her scent fresh in my mind, I wink at my crazy counterpart and head out to practice. Anton is out there flipping pucks into the air on the blade of his stick, and he winks at me, signaling that I should hit my ready stance as soon as I get into the net.

I stand with my knees bent and gloves up, and in my periphery, I see Grentley making his way toward me. However, I keep my eyes locked on the puck that Anton flips around. I feel the tension build in my body, ready to go into a butterfly when Anton lets the puck loose. He skates around the net, and I track his movements. I'm taller than Grentley by a few inches, so I know I take up a lot of space even in a ready stance. It's basically instinct for me to flip my glove toward the top corner when Anton shoots, and I close my glove around the puck with a laugh.

I've got this.

After practice, Coach asks Grentley and me to meet him in his office, so I hurry through a shower and drop off my gear with the equipment manager. I give Emerson's hat one last sniff for good luck but realize Grentley isn't in the room. I hustle to Coach's office, but Grentley isn't there either.

"Come on in, Gun." Coach rubs at his temples. "Grentley's agent threw a fit, and I met with him separately. This doesn't need to be a big deal."

"Huh. Okay." I take a seat across the desk. I hadn't thought about calling Brian about any of this. Should I be talking to my agent before I discuss lineups with Coach? "What's up, Coach?"

He taps the desk and smiles. "You're doing great out there, Gun. More and more teams are using goalie tandems nowadays."

I nod. "Sure. It's a long season." I try to remain neutral about this. I know the other guys on the team place a lot of weight into making that first line rotation. For keepers, it's more about building stamina for a whole game and keeping your head focused for all three periods.

Coach leans back, relaxing a bit. "The Fury wants to move to that flexible model, son. We believe both of you bring something special to the pipes. We're going to alternate you on this away series."

A weight melts off my shoulders as I realize I've earned a place out there. I think about the Boston goalies who embrace each other after every game, regardless of which one played on the ice. Somehow, I doubt Grentley and I are headed in that direction. "What did he have to say about that idea, sir?"

Coach hesitates and purses his lips. "Focus on your game, Gunnar."

He turns in his chair and starts clacking away at his computer, signaling to me that we are done with this conversation. I back out of the office, unsure of what it all means but eager to get home and tell Emerson what happened.

How great is that, though? I have someone at home I'm excited to talk to about work, and I'll get to hear about her experiences with the music kids, too. Things with Emerson are beginning to feel less like a cover-up ruse and more... real.

I swing by the grocery store since I know she'll be volunteering later than I'll be at the arena. She made me promise not to pick her up, like an overexcited mom at an elementary school, which is a comparison that made me laugh. I still think I should take care of her more, at least arrange for a driver or something until she learns to do it herself. But she seemed really excited about taking the bus, and who am I to deny her an adventure?

I think about the peace of mind I'll have knowing there's a planned rotation for me and Grentley in the upcoming games while I dice ginger and smash garlic to sauté with chicken and veggies for dinner. I even grabbed some salted chocolate truffles for my Salty since I know she likes that stuff. Eventually, the door opens, and she bursts in with a huge smile on her face, arms full of folders. "Oh my gosh, it smells amazing in here."

She sets the papers on the counter and peels off her coat, hanging it beside mine on a peg like even our jackets were meant to be together. And then she throws her arms around me and kisses me on the cheek. "How was your day?" Her eyes twinkle, and I can't help but laugh, feeling so damn happy and content.

"It was great. Give me a minute to dish this up, and I'll tell you about it."

She nods. "I'll run and change into my comfy pants. I want to tell you about my day, too."

She emerges a moment later in leggings and a baggy T-shirt that I think might be mine. I'm really fucking distracted by the swell of her ass in those pants. The hem of the shirt stops mid-cheek, and it's difficult for me to contain my urge to lift it and just squeeze all that beautiful butt. I clear my throat and grab our plates, bringing them around the counter and setting them out by our stools.

Emerson takes a big mouthful, groaning in delight before she swallows and tells me, "Lucia and Omar were more than happy to have me take over some of the registration paperwork." She points at the pile of folders. "A lot of kids register using paper forms, and I'm going to enter all of it into the database. I know that probably sounds boring and really basic."

I shake my head. "If it interests you, it's not boring, right?"

She beams. "I just love feeling like a part of this. These kids…if they do have a music teacher at school, it's only half an hour a week. What can they achieve with just half an hour? I'm so thrilled they can take these lessons. Some of them are doing vocals and instruments, and I love that Scale Up doesn't require them to specialize…Gunnar, it's all about the love of music and what that does to enrich their lives. Not, like, the stuffy performance culture I grew up with." She sighs and takes another bite. "I'm rambling. What made your day so good?"

I squeeze her thigh. "If that was rambling, I like it. But I'm feeling the joy in hockey right now, too." I tell her about nailing my stance and transitions today and how coach plans to rotate Grentley and me. "I'm really feeling more and more like I've earned my place out there," I admit, smiling timidly at her. "But I guess this is a trial for the away series, and I'll have to keep worrying once we're back."

The smile she reflects back at me, bright and earnest, her brown eyes shining … it makes me see why my dad and all my uncles are always talking about how amazing it is to be married.

I clear my throat, take a final bite of food, and ask her, "Have you made a decision about New York yet? I know Brian is pretty pumped for you to join me at the fan fest..."

She nods. "I did. I talked to Lucia and Omar about missing a few days. I want to be with you, to see everything." She bites her lip. "However, I don't want to see my parents. And I'd rather not to tell them I'm coming to town."

"I wouldn't expect you to call them," I shake my head. "I guess they don't follow hockey blogs or look into fan fest VIP events."

She laughs and stands, reaching for my plate, which I tuck back close to my chest. "Gunnar, you cooked. Let me wash up." I growl at her, and she laughs. "Okay, fine." She sets her plate down and fluffs her hair, sending a waft of that amazing scent my way. "And you're right. My family definitely won't come looking for the Fury at the hockey arena."

CHAPTER 24
GUNNAR

EMERSON IS ABSOLUTELY ADORABLE ON THE RIDE TO THE airport. She's meeting up with Cam and Essence to fly to New York, and I told her I'd drop her off before I head up to meet the team since we have a chartered flight.

"I've never actually stayed at the Plaza before," she says, fiddling with her purse on her lap. "I mean, why would I when I live so close, right? But it will be so much fun staying at such a fancy hotel."

I squeeze her leg as I ease over into the lane for short-term parking. I intend to escort her as far into the airport as I'm allowed. "You should have fun. I hope you book a spa treatment or something while you're there, obviously for a time when you're not watching me play." I wink at her, and she laughs.

"I can't wait to watch with the PAWs," she sighs. "Cam and Essence said they have a shirt for me for Fan Fest…"

I nod. "Yeah, Cappy mentioned they made some sort of custom *I Flame N.Y.* shirts or something with the Fury logo. I don't know."

"I love all the trash talk with sports. You're sure it doesn't hurt anyone's feelings?"

A laugh busts out of my throat. "Babe, everyone is having fun. I promise you'll see some anti-Pittsburgh shirts. You might even hear some bad language." I wink and park in the garage near the pedestrian bridge to the terminal. "You have your pre-check stuff all situated? Brian mentioned you weren't enrolled."

I was surprised she wasn't all set up for easy first-class flying since I know she travels for music. I can't imagine her snobby parents waiting in line with the peons. It's going to make me even madder if I find out they breeze through all the lines and leave her elsewhere.

Emerson smiles. "I'm all verified. Oh!" She hesitates as I hoist her bag from the back seat and tug it along the walkway. "You're coming in?"

"I want to make a sex joke right now, but I also want to make sure you find your friends."

Emerson rolls her eyes and stretches on tiptoe, scanning the security area. "Oh, there they are!" She waves. I nod my chin at Cam, who grins. "Okay, so I'll see you in a few hours? At the arena?" Emerson bites her lip, and I scoop her into my arms.

"I will see you there." I press a kiss to her forehead, loving the sigh she lets out when I do. Then, feeling brave, I bend to kiss her mouth. Just a soft little press of my lips to hers, like a husband would totally do if he was really in love with his wife. And she twists her hands in my shirt, holding me close, opening her mouth as if she's been waiting to kiss me her whole life. I pull back, breathless. "Okay, Salty, they're going to arrest us for indecency if you keep that up."

She makes a nervous sound, and I squeeze her backside. "See you soon."

I watch as she heads down the escalator to Cam and Essence and waves before breezing through the security check.

My own flight is obviously easy since we all are scanned and checked, and our equipment staff deals with all the complicated luggage, like expensive ice skates and goalie gear. I just need to show up in a suit and look good. We don't even have to check into the hotel or haul our own shit to our rooms. The bus meets us at the airport and takes us straight to the arena to change into jeans and jerseys and meet up with the fans.

I'm not going to lie—I love this. This is a controlled environment where I am prepared to be photographed, and I know nobody is taking anything out of context. These are all fans who either traveled to meet us here or root for us from another city, so that makes them all the more special.

We meet on the mezzanine level of the arena, where, tomorrow, eighteen thousand fans will line up for hot dogs and beer. Today, it's just the select thousand or so who got tickets. I realize that might be an overwhelming number of people for Emerson. I should have prepared her more that there will be tons of booths and stations where people can meet specific players, shoot inflatable pucks at fake nets, or even get a team tattoo.

I sort of hope Emerson skips the tattoo line, just because I want to be there with her when she gets her first ink. I know that's selfish, but something tells me she won't go for a Fury tat today anyway. I spy her, Cam, and

Essence sharing a bag of popcorn over by a pen full of actual puppies, and I laugh out loud. Brian must have had something to do with the organization of the event.

Sure enough, when I check my schedule, I'm up first to cuddle puppies and encourage fans to adopt from shelters. Don't mind if I do.

I make my way toward my wife and love the expression on her face when she sees me. "Hey, Salty." I toss her a wink as my handler from the team office tugs at my sleeve and steers me toward the puppies. "Come pet a dog with me."

She steps toward the pen, where a large crowd of people are squatting and squealing at the cute little dogs. "Hey, guys," I say to the crowd, both furry and human alike. "Who wants a picture?"

They're about to open the booth for fans, but I wave at the staff members. "Excuse me, Wanda? Can my wife get in first?"

She looks at the line of fans, now jumping up and down and hollering my name above the din of puppy barks. Wanda frowns.

I frown. "Wanda. She's my wife."

Wanda rolls her eyes. "Yes, fine, get her in there."

Someone opens the pen and escorts Emerson inside, where I tug her onto my knee as I kneel by the dogs. I press a kiss to her cheek as a camera flashes and dogs start licking my hands where I have them pressed against Emerson's waist. She laughs and coos, tossing her head back when one of the dogs jumps up onto her lap. The two of us stare down at the little fella, ruffing his fur while Fury staff takes a thousand pictures. This is going to make Brian cream his pants, but also it's the fucking best. My gorgeous, curvy wife is on my lap, and

I'm being loved by dogs. What on this earth could be better?

"Mr. Stag, we really need to keep things moving." Wanda's voice is firm above the din, and Emerson sighs. She rests her forehead against mine and gives the dog on our lap one final scratch.

"Love you," I blurt out, and then I freeze. Objectively, it's something I should say where people can hear it. Of course, I would love my wife. But Emerson and I haven't talked at all about feelings. And…I sort of think it's true. But that's impossible. We just met.

I look into her eyes to see if she's terrified by what I just blurted, but she smiles at me and waves. She blows me a kiss and climbs to her feet, taking all her warmth with her. I need to get it together and compose myself before Wanda starts letting the fans in here with me and the dogs.

I watch my wife walk away, because I'm never missing a chance to stare at that ass, and then I put on my game face. "All right, Fury fans," I say. "Who wants to meet a goalie?"

My hour in the puppy pen flies by, and I have a break before I'm supposed to go sit at a table to sign autographs. I wander around a bit in search of my Salty. I grin at a group of kids racing to put on goalie gear the fastest, wondering what that exhibit must smell like, but I decide they probably used brand-new gear instead of seasoned stink pads.

I consider challenging Emerson to that particular activity, but when I see her, all thoughts of enjoyment slip away like a dropped stick on the ice. Emerson is backed against a rail, a terrified expression on her face, while two people loom over her, frowning in her personal space.

I stalk toward her, my strides eating the ground until I'm close enough to hear and realize that these are her fucking parents. What would a fancy-ass conductor and his wife be doing at an exclusive hockey fan event? I approach her side just in time to hear her father sneer, "We need to talk, young lady."

CHAPTER 25
EMERSON

THE OPPRESSIVE SCENT OF MY FATHER'S COLOGNE HITS ME before his words do. It's the same thick scent he wears to conduct, to berate me during practice sessions, to tower over me at family dinners. I grip the railing behind me. I don't respond when he says we need to talk, but I glance at my mother. I don't think I was expecting warmth in her expression necessarily, but I'm stunned to see the icy fury etched into her face.

My father gestures at my shirt—the one I love matching with my new friends. He says, "What kind of outfit is this? You look like a common groupie." I don't respond that he and my mother are actually the ones who stand out here, in their finery among casual sports fans. My parents are pinch-faced and broody while everyone else is excited to be here with their heroes.

My mother hovers at his elbow, wringing her hands. "You've completely let yourself go. Have you gained weight?"

I swallow my rage and the bile that rises at her hurtful words. "What are you doing here?" My voice sounds small, as if I'm the person I was before I hopped on that train.

My father's jaw clenches. "The board meeting is tomorrow. We've spoken, and they're willing to overlook your … indiscretions…if you return now. As you know, the symphony needs a fresh, young face to weather this storm."

"I don't want—"

"What you want is irrelevant," my father snaps, stepping closer and lowering his voice. "Look at yourself. I warned you this is what comes from women playing the cello. It's indecent. Weeks spent spreading your legs for that instrument and some hockey player."

My mother touches his arm. "That's enough. Someone might hear."

My heart pounds. I can hear it, feel it in my throat. I'm going to be sick as my father snarls, "Let them hear." His face reddens. "Our daughter is debasing herself, living in sin with that overgrown—"

"Is there a problem here?"

Gunnar's voice cuts through my father's tirade. My husband positions himself at my side, slightly in front of me. He appears casual, but I can feel the tension running through his tight body. Strength radiates from Gunnar in contrast to my father's brittle anger.

"This is a private conversation." My father straightens his tie. "Family business."

"Your daughter is my wife," Gunnar's tone remains measured. "And you're making her uncomfortable."

"Wife?" Father scoffs. "That drunken Vegas spectacle hardly counts as—"

"Security?" Gunnar raises his hand, and I notice two

men in black shirts already approaching. "These people were just leaving."

"You can't dismiss me—"

"Actually, I can. This is a private event, and you're harassing one of our VIP guests." Gunnar's smile is ice cold. "We don't allow fans who disrespect our guests."

Summoned by Gunnar's mere wave, a pair of security guards appears and flanks my parents. Mom starts to protest, but Dad grabs her arm, shooting me a look of pure venom. "When you're done with this rebellion, don't expect—"

"Get them out of here," Gunnar says quietly.

I watch them disappear into the crowd, my whole body trembling. Gunnar turns to me and cups my face in his massive hands. "Hey Salty, look at me. You're safe."

"I'm so sorry," I whisper. "I never thought they'd—"

"Stop. You have nothing to be sorry for." His thumbs stroke my cheeks. "Listen to me. You don't owe them anything. Not your talent, not your time, not your life."

I lean into his touch, fighting tears. "But the board—"

"Fuck the board." He pulls me against his chest. "You're part of my team now, and I put my body on the line for my team every single day. Nobody gets to hurt you. Not even your parents."

I wrap my arms around his waist, breathing in his clean, familiar scent. Behind us, I hear the excited chatter of fans, the barking of puppies, and music pumping through speakers. This is my new world. This is my choice.

"Thank you," I murmur into his jersey.

He kisses the top of my head. "Always, Salty. Always."

· · ·

"Let's get you back to the hotel." Gunnar keeps an arm around me while texting someone. Within moments, Cam and Essence appear, their faces tight with concern. Gunnar hands me a bottle of water and briefly explains to my friends what happened. I hate that they know I'm dealing with such an embarrassing scandal. I begin to protest, wanting them to be able to enjoy this event with Banksy and Cappy, who have now also made their way over to us along with Gunnar's brothers. The twins, seeming to sense Gunnar's rage, crack their knuckles menacingly.

Gunnar waves them back, keeping one arm tightly around my shoulders. "I have to stay for team stuff, but I don't want you alone." Gunnar's thumb traces circles on my shoulder as he appeals to Cam and Essence. "Would you guys mind...?"

"Of course not." Cam wraps me in a hug, pulling me away from Gunnar's side. "We'll order room service and watch terrible movies."

Gunnar tips his chin in thanks and walks us to the edge of the festival space, pressing his forehead to mine. "I hate leaving you like this."

"I'm okay." My voice wavers. "Really."

"Liar." He kisses me softly. "I'll come straight up after the game. Don't argue—my brothers already cleared it with Coach."

"But you need rest—"

"I need to hold my wife." His eyes are fierce. "I'll rest better knowing you're safe."

Essence appears with my purse and coat. "Car's here."

"Text me when you're settled?" Gunnar cups my face. "And Salty? I meant what I said. You don't owe them anything."

. . .

The Plaza is exactly as grand as I imagined, but I hardly notice the ornate lobby. Cam and Essence hustle me straight to my room, where they immediately start raiding the mini bar.

"Tiny expensive vodka?" Cam waves a bottle.

I shake my head, curling into the plush armchair. "I should stay clear-headed."

"Fair." Essence flops onto the bed. "But we're ordering every dessert on the menu."

"And watching *The Princess Bride*," Cam adds. "Non-negotiable."

My phone buzzes with a text from Gunnar:

> Miss you already, Salty. Try to rest. I'm coming for you after we win this thing.

I clutch the phone to my chest, overwhelmed by the contrast between my old family and this new one I've stumbled into. Cam and Essence chattering about room service options. Gunnar's promise to return. Even my growing collection of Stags who've been texting support since security escorted my parents out.

"Hey." Essence tosses me the room service menu. "Choose something decadent. Doctor's orders."

"You're not a doctor."

"No, but I play one on TV," she winks. "Seriously, though, you're safe here. Let us take care of you until your man gets back."

I frown at the menu and let it fall to the bed. "You two are missing your chance to see the Fury play. I hate that. I feel like such a burden."

Essence holds up a finger. "I am exactly where I want to be, Emerson. These guys play 80 games in a season. Trust me, I'll be at the next one."

Cam nods and picks the menu up, shoving it toward me until I laugh.

I order chocolate cake and listen to them quote every line of the movie, slowly feeling the tension leave my body.

I feel my phone vibrate with another text from Gunnar:

> About to warm up. You good?

I can feel his protective energy from here, and I really do feel better. I send back:

> Safe and sound. Go win.

His response is immediate:

> Always do when I'm playing for you.

I fall asleep during the movie, waking briefly when Cam tucks a blanket around me. "Rest up, sweetie. Your knight in shining goalie pads will be here soon."

For the first time since seeing my parents, I smile.

CHAPTER 26
GUNNAR

I am a man possessed during the game against New York. At one point, I almost get into a fucking goalie fight with their center, but I secure a shutout for the Fury and hurry my ass back to my wife at the hotel. I'll pay whatever fine Coach decides...I'm not rooming with Banksy. Not when Emerson is shaken up and needs me.

I blow off a media interview and barely shower, rushing outside to grab a cab and practically sprinting through the lobby to get to the elevators and up to Emerson's room. I have the key programmed into the app on my phone, so when I slip in, I find Essence and Cam passed out on the couch in the sitting area, and I gently wake them up.

"Hey," I whisper. "Thank you both so much for staying with her."

"Of course." Cam rubs his eyes and looks at his watch. "You shouldn't be here yet." He arches a brow at me.

I grin. "I might have blown off some responsibilities and punted to your guy." I tug at my collar. "I'm not going back to my room with Banksy. Make of that what you will."

Cam ushers Essence, still half asleep, into the hall and mutters something about getting her to her room before he makes an entrance. I grin briefly but then head into the bedroom of Emerson's suite.

She's on her back with an arm over her face, breathing slow and deep. Good, asleep. Relief floods my system as I yank off my shoes and pants, toss my shirt on the floor, and crawl into bed beside her. She sighs in her sleep and curls against me, and I hold her, stroking her hair and trying not to get out of this bed to murder her asshole parents.

My phone alarm goes off around six, and Emerson groans at the noise. "You can sleep if you want," I whisper, running my fingers through the silky strands of her hair. "I'm doing the milk thing before ice time today."

She sits up. "Oh god, I forgot about your ad! You wanted me to be there."

I gradually sit, feeling the strain of last night's game in my muscles. I shouldn't have skipped a post-game massage, that's for damn sure. "Hey, Salty, you don't have to do anything that feels overwhelming. I can paint a milk mustache and look cute without you. Promise."

I wink at her, and she groans. "No," she says, crawling out of bed and treating me to a glimpse of her luscious thighs. "I can do this. I can be a sideline fan. Or whatever. A fluffer? What's my role here?"

"Babe." I stand up. "Fluffer is a completely different industry." She grins, and I shake my head, looking around for my pants. I'll have to just wear my post-game suit to the studio and hope they'll dress me how they want. I glance around the room, noticing a zillion tiny bottles in the trash and room service trays scattered everywhere. "I'm glad you had an okay night despite everything. You feeling okay?"

She laughs. "Not going to lie, I could go for a greasy egg sandwich." She walks into the bathroom and shuts the door.

The two of us get ourselves together and walk through the lobby, politely declining the doorman's offer to call a car. I crave that greasy sandwich Emerson mentioned, and she assures me she knows just the hole-in-the-wall spot to grab it, which we do en route to the studio address that Brian has texted me at least 35 times.

"Gunnar Stag here for the milk ad," I tell the security guard, and their entire demeanor changes. Em and I are escorted through the building to a bustling studio filled with bright lights, cameras, and a thousand people running around with boxes, trays, and equipment.

"Gunnar!" A young white guy with a goatee and a clipboard approaches to shake my hand…very enthusiastically. "I'm Mitch, and I'm going to get you to wardrobe. And who do we have here?" He raises an eyebrow and glances at Emerson, who smiles.

"This is my wife," I tell him.

Mitch grins. "Well, Mrs. Stag, let's get you—"

"She's Ms. Saltzer," I correct him. Emerson looks exasperated.

"Emerson," she says. "I'm just here for support."

Mitch nods. "I'm so sorry about the name mix-up.

Emerson, let's get you set up with craft services while we get this guy 'stached up."

He guides her away, and she waves as a flock of black-clad studio staff tugs me toward a dressing room. Before I can form words, I'm stuffed into fake hockey gear and a generic Fury jersey, my hair greased up to look sweaty, and a white gloopy mustache painted on my face.

Mitch claps his hands in approval at the sight of me and points a finger toward the ceiling. "This is very important, Gunnar. You must not actually drink the glass of milk when you're doing the commercial. It's not milk. Okay?"

I hear Emerson giggle from the side, and she waves at me, holding a giant glass of (apparently) actual milk. This whole place is a buffet of dairy, which makes sense. Emerson holds a plate of cheese and seems to be eyeing a giant tub of yogurt. I pat my stomach, already hungry after digesting the egg. "Babe, save me some of the Gruyere."

She nods, and, after finishing her milk, sets the glass to the side and gives me a thumbs up. I enjoy having her here and seeing her relax with the support staff. I appreciate when she's nearby because I know she's being cared for and happy.

It turns out that shooting a milk commercial is pretty easy. There will be footage of a body double in a hockey goal, saving shot after shot. Why they don't use me for that part, I'll never know, but Mitch says not to worry about it. My entire job is to act like I'm exhausted, peel my helmet off, fake-chug a glass of milk, and then slap the helmet back on. Brian says I'm not even allowed to talk on camera because that's a different set of rules, and there's an actor's union involved. Works for me.

I raise and lower the helmet a few dozen times until the director yells, "Let's wrap. Great work, Gunnar."

I hear Emerson whoop, and, apparently with Mitch's permission, she rushes toward me with a cube of cheese on a toothpick. "You look so cute." She feeds me the cheese and pecks me on the cheek.

"Okay, you two are adorable." Mitch shakes his head. "Super sweet. But Gunnar, we have another athlete coming in, so…" He drifts off, pointing toward the dressing room, and I nod, rushing to get changed and return to Emerson.

She's holding a brown paper bag, grinning, when I finish up. "That was so fun. I like the open bar. Of cheese." She hands me the bag. "I stole some Swiss for you, husband."

"Best wife ever," I joke, draping an arm around her shoulders. Once we're back outside, I pull her toward a bench and gesture for her to sit. "Can we talk about the rest of today? I want to make sure you're okay since I'll be tied up from basically now until midnight."

She purses her lips and nods, tapping her hands on her legs. "Yeah, I hate that I missed watching you play last night. It's Grentley's turn to play today, right?"

I nod. "Listen, if you want to go back home, we can arrange that. If you want to stick around, I'll make sure Cam and Essence are good to guard you with their tiny lives."

She puffs out a laugh and stares at the bustling morning traffic of the city. New York is far busier than Pittsburgh, with an angry edge to it. Or perhaps that's just my rage simmering not too far below the surface. "What are you thinking?" I squeeze her hand and look into her eyes.

She smiles and tilts her head. "You referred to Pittsburgh as home, and … it felt right. Is that weird? I've barely lived there for a month …"

"Not weird at all." I adjust my posture so I'm facing her, sitting sideways on the bench. "Having you at my place feels right. I can't imagine the apartment without you. I'm serious."

She smiles for real this time, looking up into my eyes. A sunbeam breaks through a cloud and reflects off the building behind us, bathing Emerson in a peachy glow. She's so damn beautiful that I can't help but lean in and kiss her, deeply and properly, drawing a breathy moan from her throat that I want to memorize and cherish forever.

I'm falling for this woman. Hard. I know it in every fiber of my being. Then I remember that what we have is precarious, built on impulsive, reckless mistakes. I exhale slowly through my nose. "What are you thinking?"

She bites her bottom lip, her teeth digging into the plump, delicious flesh. "There's a lot I could accomplish today with Scale Up. It might help me feel more grounded if I stay busy. I hate missing your game, but …"

I draw her in tight and press a hand to her head. "Salty, whatever you need. Always. You come first, okay?" She nods against my shirt, and I hold her for a few more minutes before pulling out my phone to call Brian, who immediately sets some plans in motion to get her back to Pittsburgh.

We go to the hotel, gather her things, and I wait with her until the black sedan rolls up to take her to the airport. I kiss her more thoroughly than I ought to in public, and I'm fairly certain some people take pictures of us, but what the hell do I care if others see me making out with my wife?

Morning skate is terrible. I'm distracted, and Coach is pissed. I ride the bench the entire game while Grentley secures us another shutout. Nobody asks me to stick around for media interviews, so I take my sweet ass time in the shower and wait for the team bus. We're flying back tonight, so no one goes out to get wasted before our next series of home games.

Fine by me. The sooner I get back to my wife, the better.

I pull out my phone to call her from my seat on the bus, and my heart skips a beat when I see my notifications.

FURY AND FLAMES: HOCKEY'S HOTTEST SCANDAL

BuzzLine Sports Exclusive

Star Pittsburgh goalies Gunnar Stag and Ashley Weber have been spotted getting cozy at multiple league events, raising eyebrows across the NHL. Sources close to Weber's husband, Boston netminder Jack Thompson, suggest that his recent slump may be linked to tension both in the crease and at home. The Fury's rising star Stag, despite his recent marriage to NYC socialite Emerson Saltzer, has been photographed engaging in "intense conversations" with Weber at charity events and post-game meetups. "Their chemistry is undeniable," says one source who wishes to remain anonymous. "It's not just about hockey." The league office has expressed concerns regarding professional conduct, especially given Thompson's position as Boston's franchise player. Representatives for all parties declined to comment, but one thing is clear: this season's goalie matchups just became a lot more personal.

RELATED:

Thompson's Save Percentage Drops Amid Personal Drama

Who is Emerson Saltzer? The Maestro's Daughter Making Waves

Top 10 NHL Power Couples

I nearly choke on my own saliva reading that absolute garbage of a "news" story, but I don't have long to simmer over it because Brian starts calling.

"Yeah." I don't even bother with a greeting, and he doesn't waste any time on small talk.

"G Stag, we might be fucked. You need to tell me if there's anything to this."

I tug on my hair with my free hand. "Jesus, Brian. Of course not. You have to know I'm gone for Emerson, man. Fuck."

He hums. "That's interesting. Okay. Well, this is going to get worse before it gets better."

I kick the seat in front of me, thankfully not hard enough to damage it or my foot. "Brian, I can handle this and any fallout, but I don't want Emerson dragged into this. Do you know her parents came to the fan fest last night and screamed at her? It was disgusting."

He gasps, which is super unusual for him as he's more prone to cursing and yelling at his staff. "Oy vey, Gunnar, you need to alert me when these things happen. Remember, I can take care of anything I know about in advance. Why didn't you tell me they came to the arena?"

"I don't know, man, I was a little focused on getting them the hell away from my wife."

The team begins to file onto the bus, and half of them are staring at me. I flip off the twins, but they sit in the seats directly in front of me, turned around and staring while I talk to our shared agent.

Brian sighs. I can just imagine him pinching the bridge of his nose and shaking his head. "Gunnar, this isn't good, dude. I received some intel that the source had really specific information about you and Emerson. Now I find out her parents crashed your fan fest?" He's likely about to start chugging Tums.

"What are you getting at, Brian?"

"Gunnar, I'm going to need some time with this. I'll speak to the coaching staff, but please promise me that you and Emerson will avoid any contact with her parents. Expect calls in the morning."

"Yeah." I stare at my brothers, who have their phones in hand and eyebrows raised. They know. I guess word is out. "Thanks, Brian."

He begins yelling into his other phone before he even hangs up with me. It's a long and miserable journey back to Pittsburgh.

CHAPTER 27
EMERSON

I hate leaving Gunnar in New York for the second Fury game of that series, but everything happening with my parents has me so shaken up that I know coming back to Pittsburgh is the right choice. *Home...*

I told Gunnar that I needed to go home. It makes no sense to me that I've mentally classified the apartment in Lawrenceville as "home," yet every time I even think about that space, I feel a warm, safe glow. Gunnar lived there only a few months prior to me moving in, so we have truly been creating it as a home together. The moment he thinks of something I might like or need, he orders it, and it appears. Cozy blankets on the couch, apple slicers, and even a toilet paper subscription…it all arrives with no strings attached, without comment.

I try to make him comfortable, too, cleaning up when he cooks (if he lets me) and making sure the fridge is stocked with his favorite lean protein. Somehow, this ruse, intended to help him play the game he loves, has turned into something very meaningful and real.

I take a car from the airport directly to Scale Up, and

Omar appears relieved to see me walk in the door. Roughly forty young kids swarm in between the music rooms, loudly tooting on out-of-tune instruments while waiting for the previous hour's lessons to somehow wrap up amidst the chaos.

I halt in my tracks as a young viola player spies me and starts running my way. "Miss Emerson!" The girl's name is Ilan, and the plastic beads on her braids clack as she hurries to me.

"Walking feet with your instrument," I tell her, keeping my voice calm and low.

"Oh. Right." She bites her lip and slows her pace, pausing in front of me and bouncing up and down. "I got a dress for the concert! It's purple!"

"Oh, that sounds gorgeous." I squat so we are eye to eye. "And you can move your arms easily wearing it? It's not too tight?"

She grins and nods, explaining that her mother has the little concert wardrobe card I made for the kids, explaining what to look for in performance clothes. I absolutely love that Scale Up doesn't require all black. The music school partnered with a local boutique so the kids can benefit from a sliding scale fee structure for attire. It's been so fun emailing back and forth with the youth buyer, talking about designs that might help or hinder a young trombone player differently from a flutist.

"Ilan, have you tuned your instrument yet? Want to show me your stuff?"

She takes a deep breath. "The pegs are so hard to turn."

I nod. "Maybe we can manage the fine-tuning dials near the bridge. Let's hear what you've got."

We stand to the side as she plucks the strings. She pauses and plucks again. "Sharp?" I nod, and she grins, adjusting the metal dial on her C string. Ilan tunes the instrument on her own, pausing to check with me a few times but never requiring help.

"I'm so proud of you. You've learned to do that so well, despite all this background noise." Ilan beams at her instrument as the earlier ensemble musicians file out of their rooms. The halls are chaotic for a few minutes, with Lucia directing traffic like an elite conductor.

Once all the children are in their classrooms, she rushes toward me. "We thought you wouldn't be back for a few days! Is everything all right?" She rubs my upper arm, her expression etched with concern.

I wave a hand. "There was some drama with my parents. I thought it would do me good to get back here and focus on the kids."

Lucia's brows furrow, but she nods her head. "Okay. Well, obviously, we are thrilled to have you here. What do you want to work on today?"

My mouth drops open. "Oh, whatever you need the most help with. Really! I'm on cloud nine just being here." And it's true. I might not be earning a salary, and who even knows if my name appears anywhere on any documentation for this place. There's no prestige. There are no critics raving about me in any capacity. Yet, I've never felt better.

Lucia grins. "I want you to focus on the thing that makes your heart soar, Emerson. Go on, tell me."

I take a deep breath and shake my shoulders. "Cello lessons. I'd love to help teach cello."

Lucia turns her head toward the room, emitting some deep squawks. "Go on, then, girl!"

. . .

Two hours later, I'm soaring. I've taught a dozen children to rosin their bows, perfect their grip on the neck of their instruments, and play a pizzicato version of Hot Cross Buns. My fingers are tingling, itching to make music as I hop aboard the bus home. I've never felt so inspired, so needed, and so valued.

This is my calling, I just know it.

The apartment feels empty without Gunnar, but he'll be in late tonight. I should check the game on TV, but I need to play my cello. It's been too long.

I rush into the spare room, smiling at the glow of our new sconces illuminating Gunnar's most valued medals and trophies along two of the walls while my sheet music and supplies fill the others. I never made it to my parents' house to retrieve my stash, but between the Scale Up library and my meager savings, I've managed to gather what I need to create a proper home music studio. Apart from the soundproofing, but Gunnar doesn't seem to mind.

I take a seat on the bench and begin to play, tuning my instrument carefully and working through a series of warm-ups that the children used today at Scale Up. Then I begin playing one of my own compositions—the piece I was working on the night I met Gunnar.

I work through it a dozen times, perfecting the bridge and leaning into the melody. When I open my eyes, my bow hovering over the strings, allowing the final note to echo through the room. I see my husband standing in the doorway. His face is an unreadable blend of sadness and wonder, and when he realizes I've finished, he rushes toward me, sinking to his knees.

Shirtless and barefoot, Gunnar is about as close to perfection as possible in a pair of gray sweatpants. "Salty, you are so fucking talented," he says by way of greeting. His hands are on my leg as he kneels at my side, staring into my face. "I could listen to you play for hours."

I smile at him, realizing something as I say it. "I was playing for you. I wrote that song for you."

His eyes go wide, and the pressure of his hand on my leg increases. "You wrote that for me? Really?"

I nod. "Yes. I just didn't know it."

He reaches for the cello and then pauses, hand in the air, looking to me for permission. "Will you show me? How it works?"

A surge of joy zips through my body. "Oh, I'd love that. Here, you sit." I leap to my feet, the neck of the instrument in one hand. I pat the bench, and Gunnar takes a seat, looking at me quizzically. He is tense everywhere, and I think I see a bruise blooming on one pectoral. I suppose that's part of the job in professional hockey.

Gunnar hesitates to take the instrument from me. I walk behind him, reaching over his shoulder with my mouth near his ear. Now that I've worked out all the pent-up music in my body, I'm starting to want to do other things ... with Gunnar. "Spread your legs around the instrument," I tell him. He looks over his shoulder but does as I ask. I nod. "Now grip the neck with your left hand."

He wiggles the fingers of his right hand, and I place my hand over his, guiding him toward the strings. "We're going to pluck the strings. You can be firm. It won't hurt them."

He looks at me and gives a feeble flick. Nothing really happens. I nod, and Gunnar gives the D string a good tug. He grins as the sound echoes through the room. "Hey!"

He plucks it again. "How much does this guy cost, anyway?" Another pluck.

I explain from my place behind him, "First of all, she's a lady. Look at her curves."

"Okay, fair." He plucks a different string.

"Second," I place my hands on his shoulders, leaning over to whisper, feeling a little sultry, especially as I inhale the scent of his soap, deodorant, and the fresh Gunnar scent I've missed all day. "This cello would cost $13,000 new."

"Thirteen G? Jesus, Salty." He jumps to his feet. "You can't let me fuck around with this. I'll break it. I'm a caveman."

I laugh. "You won't break it. You were doing great. Surely, you have expensive gear, too. It's made well, I promise."

He shakes his head and extends the cello toward me. "Please, babe. Take it back from me."

I slide the cello from his grasp, and he sits on the bench, shaking his head. I bite my lip, inspired, and settle myself between his legs. He sucks in a breath as I wriggle my ass back against his crotch and I feel the heavy length of him thicken against my lower back. "I can still show you things," I tell him.

He nods, his mouth very close to my ear, his breath tickling my hair. "See how I rest her against my shoulder?" Another nod as I rest my own head against his. "Her neck settles perfectly between my thumb and forefinger, and I can curve my hand around, placing my fingers exactly where they need to be along her length."

Catching on to my unspoken game, Gunnar cups the back of my neck in one of his hands, his fingers trailing sparks along my jaw. I slowly pluck out a few notes, reaching down toward the bridge and telling him, "This tiny piece of maple is vital. It's so fine, so strong, holding up the strings to make the perfect sound." As I pluck the strings, Gunnar slides his hands along my sides, fingers wrapping around to pinch my nipples when they harden into peaks inside my shirt.

"Salty, this is so fucking hot." I nod, agreeing. He nuzzles his scruffy jaw along my neck, and nothing has ever felt better. I pluck a chord of appreciation. "I'm so hard for you."

I wriggle my hips to let him know I'm very aware of that reality. My body sings under his attention. I don't know if it's because he's a particularly good lover or if I was just placed on this earth to respond to him, but heat builds in my core. I start to fidget as my legs spread around the cello, and Gunnar wraps his palms around my thighs.

I wish I could see how we look together, him spread behind me, me wrapped around this instrument, leaning back against his warm chest. "Gunnar." His name is a whisper, as close to a prayer as I know. "Make love to me."

CHAPTER 28
GUNNAR

EMERSON LAYS HER CELLO ON ITS SIDE ON THE FLOOR AND spins, wrapping those thick thighs around my waist instead of the wooden instrument. We kiss like that, perched on the black bench with my hands on her ass and her hands cupping my face. It's as if we can't possibly get close enough to one another, and I never want to be apart from her ever again.

I meant it when I told her I loved her at the fan fest. I just need to find the courage to tell her I was serious then, but I also have to tell her a lot of things that have happened since that moment.

With a low grunt, I stand, carrying her toward my bedroom. Our bedroom. Fuck that guest room bullshit—I want her in my bed with me every night. But especially right now as she writhes and wriggles in my arms.

I use my shoulder to turn the light on in my room and stride toward the bed, lowering us both and sinking into Emerson. She smiles against my lips. "I missed you," she says, nails tracing along my skin, drawing a circle around the bruise that's surfacing near my Stag tattoo.

"I missed you so bad," I echo, fumbling to get her annoying shirt up and out of the way so I can feel all that skin pressed against mine. She's got a stupid bra on, too, and I growl a little, trying to get that out of the way as well. Finally, she's bare to me, and I can see her.

She brings one hand to her neck, and I'm worried she's going to try to cover up like she did the first time we were together, but she traces her nipple, licking her lips and staring at me like she's starving and I'm hot meat. "Ha." I puff out a laugh and then dive onto her breast, kneading the amazing tissue and licking that stiff, puffy nipple until she moans.

Emerson starts jerking her hips against my crotch, where I'm stiff and leaking pre-cum all over my sweats. "You're so big, Gunnar. You feel so solid. I … can you take these off?" She snaps my waistband with one hand and tugs at my hair, pulling me up and off her nipple with a wet pop. I nod and draw back just enough to kick my pants out of the way. She peels her own off in the process.

The smile she sends once we're both naked and I'm settled back in her body—she could melt the ice a thousand times. "I love that you called this home," I tell her, kissing my way all along her stomach and sides, hands busy with her breasts.

"I love being here with you," she responds, her own hands tracing my nipples in a way I had no idea I enjoyed until right now. "Gunnar, I'm so…I need…" She arches and wiggles, moving her legs and trying to line her pussy up with my cock.

I purr, which should sound or feel weird but doesn't. "You need to come, don't you, Salty?"

She nods. "I need you. Please."

"Oh, baby, you don't ever need to beg me." I slide a

hand between us. Her pussy is soaked and I slide my finger through her arousal, making her gasp and moan. I give her clit a rub with my thumb, sliding my finger inside her channel, feeling her soft heat pulsing around me. This incredible woman is trusting me with her first sexual experiences. I'm committed to making it nice for her. Memorable in a good way.

"Gunnar! Yes!" I rub just a little bit faster, really only a few flicks. She must have been really keyed up from what we did in the music room because Emerson comes hard, so much faster than I expected. I love the sound of my name on her lips, and I can barely contain myself as she pulses around my fingers. "I want you inside me. Please?"

I nod, withdrawing my hand to reach for the condoms in my nightstand, but she puts a hand on my wrist. "I want *you*, Gunnar. Just you."

My eyes fly wide. I've never been inside a woman bare before. Ever. I grew up with parents who prepared a Safe and Satisfied basket stuffed with condoms and lube and vibrating cock rings, spermicide packs and even dental dams.

But this woman is my wife. "Salty, baby, you know I'm healthy. And I know you are, too. But ... are you on birth control?"

She shakes her head. "I'm not. But I don't care, Gunnar. I want everything with you. Every part of you. I want to feel you with nothing between us."

"Fuucckk." It should terrify me that this woman wants me to come inside her potentially fertile body, but honestly, it's hotter than ever. "Okay. If you're sure?" I brace myself on my forearms, lining my dick up with her pussy, feeling the wet glide of our bodies. There isn't anything rational about us, and it isn't just sex brain for me. I've been having forever thoughts since I met her. I want it all with Emerson. I want our house together, our lives together. I want her at my side at Stagsgiving. I want her whether I ever play another second of pro hockey or have to go back to college and get an office job instead.

"I'm so sure, Gunnar. Please. I want you." She arches her back, lining the tip of me perfectly with her opening, and I slide inside, just a little at first.

I meet her gaze, which is fixed on mine. She seems okay with this intrusion into her body, so I ease in more and more until…we're joined together. We both gasp, and I stare down at the place where our bodies connect.

"Oh shit, look at your pussy taking my cock, Emerson. God that's so fucking hot. You're taking me so good, baby."

"Gunnar!" She drops her hands to my ass, pulling me further into her body. I'm fully seated, pubic bone resting against hers, and I kiss her, reveling in the feel of our bodies connected.

Her tongue slides into my mouth, and she starts to move, so I join her, rolling my hips. I can already tell which movements make her squeak and which ones make her groan deeply. I feel the small muscle contractions when she draws in a sharp breath, and I take note when her eyes fly wide at the press of my fingers against her nipples.

"Gunnar, I feel so full! This is amazing. Is it always like this?" She's gulping in air now, sweating as she moves with me.

I laugh, holding still as she rocks and glides beneath me, finding what feels good for herself. "Gunnar, I'm going to come again. Touch me, please." And I do, balancing myself on just one arm now as I reach for her clit and press down while I hammer into her faster and harder, deeper and longer until I feel that fantastic rippling pulse of her orgasm.

"Emerson, holy shit this feels incredible. Baby, nothing has ever felt so good. God damn!" I grunt and seize above her, balls tightening as a huge blast of release spurts into her body again and again. I'm panting, kissing her with all that I have, sinking into her arms. This is perfection. This is us.

And then I remember why I was so worked up on the trip home. I remember the headlines. I remember what the tabloids are saying about me and Ashley, as if I'd ever dream of being unprofessional with another hockey player. As if I'd ever, ever treat my wife with such disrespect. "Emerson." I'm still panting, still inside her amazing body. "Emerson, I have to tell you something."

CHAPTER 29
EMERSON

THE WORLD NARROWS TO JUST GUNNAR AND ME IN THIS moment - our bodies still joined, his weight a delicious anchor. I've never felt so complete, so utterly safe. My fingers trace the muscles of his back, memorizing every dip and curve. For once in my life, I'm exactly where I'm meant to be.

Which is why I notice immediately when his body tenses.

"Emerson." His voice is rough, strained. "I have to tell you something."

My heart skips. He brushes my hair away from my face, his blue eyes serious. The tenderness of his touch somehow makes whatever is coming worse. "What's wrong?"

"There's something in the press... about me and Ashley."

"The women's team goalie?" He nods. The warmth drains from my body despite our connection, what we just shared. I think of seeing them together - their easy rapport and shared understanding of the game. But I know

Gunnar. He sees her as a peer, a colleague. "Wait." I try to sit up, and he rolls to the side to let me. "They're implying that you ..." I trail off, unable to finish the sentence. But he catches my meaning.

"It's completely false," he rushes to add. "Complete bullshit. They're saying we've been... that we've been meeting up. That it's affecting her husband's game."

I try to process this while he explains the tabloid article about Thompson's slump, and the league's concerns. Part of me wants to pull away and cover myself, but Gunnar pulls me closer as if he can protect me from this with just his body alone. Like always, his touch centers me. However, the revelation is upsetting.

"I think Brian is thinking..." Gunnar hesitates, and I feel his heart pounding against my side. "Brian believes your father might be feeding this to the press."

"My father?" The words come out hollow. Of course, he would. Of course, he'd try to destroy this, too. This beautiful thing I've found, this man who makes me feel safe and valued - my father would never let me keep it. He sees me as a threat to his work, so he's trying to take away my Gunnar.

"Hey, look at me." Gunnar cups my face, and I feel the wetness of his palms. I'm crying. "Brian is already working on it. We can fight this."

I shake my head, finally shifting away from him. This is why I can't have nice things. I can't choose my instrument. I never chose my college major or my occupation. The things I choose bring about destruction. I look into my husband's eyes, so steady and intense, focused on me. "Your career, your endorsements... this is exactly what my father wants. To prove that I ruin everything I touch."

"Salty, please." I back away from him and climb out of

the bed. He reaches for me, but I'm already wrapping myself in the sheet. "Don't do this. Don't let him win."

"I'm toxic to your career, Gunnar. The hospital deal, the milk campaign - everything you've worked for..." My voice breaks as I think of how my presence threatens all of it.

"Then we'll figure something else out. Please, just... talk to my mom first." He stands up, his eyes pleading. "She's been through this - when she and Dad were dating, the press tried to say all kinds of crap about their relationship. She knows how to handle it. She's a lawyer, Em. She can help."

I think of Juniper's warmth and her quiet strength. The way she brought me soup and sat with me through movies. But I also think of the headlines and how Gunnar's reputation is being torn apart because of me, as well as my father's ruthless determination to control every aspect of my life. Gunnar has a large, supportive family, and he's bringing me into it while I drag scandal behind me like a virus.

"I can't let you lose everything because of me." I gather my clothes, hands shaking.

"The only thing I'd lose is you." His voice cracks. "And that would destroy me more than any scandal."

I want to believe him. God, I want to believe him. But I can already see tomorrow's headlines and imagine the whispers in the locker room. My father won't stop until he wins - he never has. He'll keep coming for Gunnar, keep trying to destroy him until I give in.

"I need some time to think," I whisper, clutching my clothes to my chest. "I need..."

"Emerson." He sounds desperate now. "At least talk to my mom. Please. Let me call her."

I pause at the door, not looking back because I know if I do, I'll crumble. "I'll think about it."

But we both know I'm already planning my escape. I will have to disappear for real this time, somewhere else. There must be some place outside my family's influence. My father has always known exactly how to hurt me - by hurting the people I love. And I love Gunnar too much to let that happen.

The thought stops me cold. I love him. Really, truly love him.

Which is exactly why I have to leave.

For now, however, I retreat to the guest room and climb into the cold bed alone. I lie there, staring at the ceiling, wondering how I ever fooled myself into believing this life was something I could attain.

CHAPTER 30
GUNNAR

It absolutely killed me not to follow Emerson to the other room last night. She said she needed space to think. Respecting that was probably harder than any conversation I'm about to have with Coach. I pace the apartment living room at dawn, already dressed for morning skate. My phone is pressed to my ear as I beg, "Mom, please. I'm worried she'll disappear if I leave her alone."

"Of course I'll come over." Mom's voice is steady, calming. "But honey, Emerson's not her parents. She chose to leave them. She chose you."

"I know, but—" I break off as I hear movement in the hall. Emerson emerges from the guest room, circles under her eyes matching mine. She freezes when she sees me.

"I'll be there in twenty minutes," Mom says. "Go to practice. Let me handle this."

I end the call and watch Emerson drift toward the coffee maker. "My mom's coming over."

She nods, not meeting my gaze. "You don't have to have someone babysit me. I won't talk to the media."

"It's not—" I step toward her, but she flinches. "Please

just talk to her. She knows about dealing with hockey press."

Another nod. I want to grab her, hold her, and make her understand that none of this matters compared to losing her. But I've never felt so helpless. I swallow a giant lump in my throat. Fuck this. The two of us always connect physically. "Emerson, I need a hug," I tell her, dropping my bag to the floor and holding out my arms. "Please?"

Her face shifts to a more familiar expression. Not exactly happy, but less miserable. She steps into my arms and melts against me as I hold her tightly. I inhale the scent of her hair and murmur into it, "I need a replacement hat soon for my locker. The one I have is running out of Salty smell."

"Gunnar." She pulls her head back and looks into my face. "How can you be thinking of smelly hats right now?"

I shrug and pull her close again. "Because all I think about is you, babe. You and I ... we are special. In the end, we will come through this and all the bullshit will fade away. I know it."

Her voice is muffled against my shirt, and I loosen my grip just a little so she can repeat whatever she said. "I wish I had your confidence about it."

I kiss the tip of her nose. "I will inject confidence into you all evening if you'd like." She smacks my chest. However, the crass joke has the desired effect of cutting the tension a bit. "Please be here when I get back. Please?"

She blinks away tears and nods, and I kiss her on the cheek before grabbing my things and heading out the door. I just hope my mom arrives at the apartment before Emerson decides to bolt. For once, I'm relieved that she doesn't drive.

. . .

My own drive to practice is a blur. I'm barely inside the door when the twins materialize beside me.

"These haters are out of their minds," Tucker says, flipping off his phone and throwing it in his cubby.

"Total bullshit," Alder adds. "Everyone knows you're gone for Salty."

I start suiting up, grateful for their presence. "Brian thinks her father planted it."

"Fucking hell." Tucker slams his locker shut. "That's some next-level toxic shit. Not to mention, Ashley and Thompson never did anything to deserve that. That's really fucked up, man."

I nod. The three of us work on our pads, but the twins are finished well before me since they have less gear.

"Want us to have a talk with Em's dad?" Alder cracks his knuckles. "Set the record straight?"

Despite everything, I almost smile. "Let's not add assault charges to this mess."

Grentley's sneer cuts through our conversation. "Trouble in paradise, Stag?" He stalks into the room, leaning against his locker, already suited up.

"Not now, man." I focus on my gear.

"Just saying, if you can't handle the pressure, maybe you should step back. Let someone more...professional take the net."

My brothers tense, but I keep my voice steady. "My game speaks for itself."

"Does it?" Grentley pushes off his locker. "Because all I'm hearing is drama about you and Weber. Real professional, going after a married woman—"

Tucker lunges, but I grab his arm. "He's not worth it."

"Listen to your brother, little Stag," Grentley smirks. "Wouldn't want any more bad press."

I can't take his shit for another second, but I know I can't lay a hand on him like I typically would if another hockey player pissed me off. Not under this kind of scrutiny. "What the hell's your problem, man? We're on the same team."

He huffs, a derisive, sarcastic sound. "You're like a fart, Stag. Wafting in, causing chaos. Gone a few minutes later." He bangs his stick on the ground for emphasis and stalks out of the locker room.

Practice is brutal. Every save feels like warfare, and every missed shot feels like failure. Not to mention, each time Grentley and I switch off, he either spits at me or mutters shit about me having a wandering dick. Coach's whistle finally ends the torture, and then Brian's waiting by my locker.

"We need to talk." He jerks his head toward the office. "Coach wants to meet."

I strip off my gear in silence while Brian paces. "Look, kid. This could go either way. Coach might bench you to avoid drama, or—"

"I don't care." The words surprise us both. "I mean, I care about hockey. But Emerson matters more."

Brian studies me. "You really love her, don't you?"

"Yeah." I finish taking off my pads. "I do."

Brian sniffs. "I wasn't expecting that, kid." He sniffs again. "I think you have to shower, G Stag. Hop to it. I'll work on some shit while you're in there." He shakes his phone at me and starts tapping away at the screen. I hurry to scrub myself off and then yank on some team sweats.

Brian slides his phone back in his pocket, and we make our way to Coach's office.

When we enter, the massive, balding man is behind his desk, looking grim. "Sit down, Stag."

I do. Brian hovers by the door—coach grunts.

"Here's the thing." Coach leans forward. "You're playing solid hockey. Better than I've seen. But this press shit? It's fucking with my strategy. I can't have my goalies distracted by tabloid drama."

"I understand, sir."

"Do you? Because I want to keep starting you. I want this rotation to be a permanent thing. But I need the drama to stop."

I meet his eyes. "With all due respect, sir, my marriage isn't negotiable. If that costs me ice time—"

"Jesus, kid." Coach actually laughs. "I'm not asking you to leave your wife. I'm asking you to help me manage this circus." I squint, still not quite understanding.

"I swear to you, I'm keeping my head down off the ice. It's just that my wife has people out to get her…"

Coach crosses his arms over his chest. "Well, we have to get in front of those people so they stop impacting my people. Got me?"

I nod, feeling miserable. The press and their projected image of me has dictated a lot about my life for the past month. It's exhausting. I don't want to do it anymore. I want to play hockey, make love to my wife, and maybe cuddle some damn dogs. I listen as Coach reiterates that I need to focus on my mental game, especially if I want to maintain this tandem goalie rotation. He says, "Brian has some ideas about getting ahead of the story. Are you in?"

I think of Emerson, alone and hurting, and of my brothers, ready to fight for me. My mother is probably making Emerson tea right now and sharing war stories about hockey culture.

"I'm in. But Emerson comes first."

Coach nods. "That's fine. Now let's figure out how to shut these vultures up so I can focus on winning some damn games."

Brian cracks his knuckles and steps forward but doesn't sit. "First step is getting in front of this. The milk campaign is actually perfect timing."

"How so?" I lean forward, interested despite my exhaustion. Coach growls, clearly not wanting to talk about milk or anything off-ice.

"Family-focused ads with you and Emerson. Show the real story - young couple, whirlwind romance, now supporting each other's dreams. Her work with those music kids? Golden. And Ashley's husband is willing to go on record saying this is all bullshit."

Coach grunts approval. "Thompson's a stand-up guy."

"We need to be strategic, though." Brian pulls out his phone. "I think we do day-in-the-life posts nonstop. Show Emerson at that music school, you visiting the hospital kids. Real stuff, not staged PR garbage."

I purse my lips. "I have zero time to be posting to social media."

Brian snorts. "Obviously, G-Stag. We have people for that. Hell, the Fury has people for that." Coach nods in agreement.

I scratch at my patchy beard. "I don't think Emerson wants to put the kids in the spotlight that way. It's kind of creepy, right? Plus who even knows if those kids have photo releases and shit."

Brian rolls his eyes. "We can take care of the paperwork, baby. Better than hiding. Plus..." Brian grins. "Those orchestra board members who've been hassling your father-in-law? They're very interested in hearing about innovative music education programs. Especially programs with gender parity and diverse performers."

I start to see where he's going. "You want to use Scale Up to hit back at her father?"

"Sometimes the best defense is shining a light on good work." Brian stands. "But first, you need to make sure your wife is on board. None of this works if she's not all in."

I nod, already reaching for my phone. "I need to get home."

"Go." Coach waves me off. "Sort your shit out. I need my goalie focused. Remember, G Stag. Grentley is focused as fuck."

As I head for the door, Brian calls after me. "And G Stag? We're scheduling a puppies and pucks charity event next week. Hard to look like a homewrecker when you're adopting shelter dogs with your wife."

For the first time since seeing that article, I actually smile. "Now that... that might actually work."

CHAPTER 31
EMERSON

I sit on the couch in Gunnar's jersey and boxer briefs, clutching the mug of coffee his mom thrust into my hands along with a shot of whiskey. "It'll help, I promise," she says, treating her mug to the same booster.

I should be embarrassed to be sitting here so unkempt in front of this woman, but I'm so tired from lying awake all night reeling over how my relationship with Gunnar feels so good, but it stands to derail everything Gunnar has worked so hard to achieve.

Juniper grabs a bakery bag and her coffee, then sits with me, staring into my face as she takes a long sip of her drink. "First things first, I know my son, and he's absolutely gone for you. I don't understand why he waited so long to bring you into our lives and share you, but anyone who knows him can see that he has taken the puck of his heart and slammed it into the back of your net. Or something."

I choke out a laugh. "Did you just make a hockey metaphor? Is there a goalie, or am I just…a net?"

She rolls her eyes and rummages in the bag, pulling out a scone and gesturing with it as if it's a pointer. "You know what I mean. And while I won't pretend to know you super well yet, I think I might be correct in saying that you care about Gunnar, too." She arches a brow and waits for my confirmation.

It flows naturally. "Yes. I love him." I haven't said that out loud, and as soon as I do, I wish that Gunnar had been the first to hear me speak those words. But there's more to the story, unfortunately. "I just don't see how I can stay with him without ruining his life."

I start to cry as soon as I give voice to the worry that's kept me up all night, wondering how my father managed to worm his way into this world I've chosen, where the stuffy attitudes of the Upper East Side are far away. The people around me care most about helping each other be themselves.

Seeing my distress, Juniper places her coffee mug on the floor and scoots down the couch, drawing me into her arms. She wraps me in a firm embrace that feels so different from the hugs Gunnar gives. "Hey," she pats my hair. "Gunnar's life is far from ruined. He's got a big web of people making sure that doesn't happen." I cry harder as I listen to her reassurance. I don't know what to make of this- of kindness and promises of support.

"But my father!" I sniff and notice I'm getting tears and snot on her shirt, but she glances down and then into my eyes.

"Honey, I have four sons who play elite sports. I'm not afraid of snot." She places a firm finger under my chin and tilts my face up. "And I'm not afraid of your father. Do you really think my husband is intimidated by yours? We already have our lawyer going after him for defamation and libel. Gunnar's agent has sent his research to Tim's legal team. Okay?"

My heart races and sputters as if my body cannot accept that there are forces in the world greater than my father's influence. I close my eyes and take some deep breaths. Juniper rubs my shoulders. "That's it, Emerson. Let's get you calmed down." She sits with me as I breathe, and when I open my eyes, she hands me the coffee again, which I accept. Juniper watches me while finishing her own drink. "Do you have someone you talk to? Professionally?"

I arch a brow in confusion.

She nods her head. "I work in family law. The people who come before my bench are dealing with a lot of complicated issues at home, like divorce, abuse, neglect-you name it." I sink back into the arm of the couch, physically retreating from those uncomfortable words I'm hesitant to associate with. Juniper taps her fingers on her leg. "One thing I do is connect everyone with social services, mental health professionals, and support groups. It helps more than you might realize." She smiles. "I'd love to recommend some folks I think you'd click with. Would that help you process all this change?"

My mouth is dry when I open it to speak. I shake my head. "I don't know. That all sounds really serious."

Juniper spits out a laugh. "There's nothing more serious to me than someone threatening my family, and that includes you, dear. I'm going to leave some names on the counter. What's on your plate today?"

I scrunch up my face, trying to think. "I know I was going to help with some Scale Up classes later…"

Juniper stands and slaps her thighs. "Well, that means

we have a few hours to make some calls and try to get something scheduled for you, right?"

I think about my discomfort with this idea and my reluctance to bare my soul to a stranger. Although I just met this woman, but I trust her because I trust Gunnar. Juniper believes therapy could help me feel better and navigate the turmoil happening outside my relationship.

I owe it to Gunnar to try this. I'm not sure why my stupid instinct was to run away … to where? With what resources? I take a shaking breath. "Okay," I tell my mother-in-law. "I'll give it a shot."

Juniper urges me to shower and clean up while she checks her contacts, and by the time I re-enter the kitchen, she has a short list of a few names. She offers to stay and support me when I start making calls, but I don't want to take up all her valuable time, and I really don't want to make these calls in front of anyone else, so she heads out with a promise to check in throughout the day.

I leave voicemails for the first two women on Juniper's list, but I'm taken aback when someone answers the phone on my third try.

"This is Zara. How may I help?"

"Oh." I cough. "Hi. I was hoping to check if you're accepting new patients…clients." My voice wavers.

"Yes, I am." The therapist sounds excited. "Would you like to do a brief intake now? I had a cancellation this morning."

"Oh." I grip the phone tighter. "I don't know what that entails."

"Well," Zara responds, "how about you tell me what brings you to therapy, and we can start from there?"

"I…" I glance down the hall to the trophy-cello room, thinking of Gunnar. "I recently got married. Sort of impulsively. And it's bringing up a lot of…family stuff."

"Hm. I see. Do you want to elaborate a little?"

"My father is very controlling," I admit, licking my lips and standing to pace the apartment as I talk. "He's trying to sabotage my marriage by spreading rumors to damage my husband's career. I was considering leaving my husband to make my father stop, but …" I swallow hard. "I don't want to do that. And I'm scared of what will happen if I stay."

I hear the scratch of pen on paper in the background, and Zara's voice is pointed when she asks, "Are you physically safe right now? Tell me more about being scared."

"I'm safe." I feel the truth of it as I say the words. "I'm physically safe. My husband and his family say they have everything under control with lawyers. But I'm not accustomed to feeling this way."

Zara hums again in the silence after my confession. "Not used to feeling safe?"

I nod, remembering she can't see me, and say, "Right. I'm … I've always been on edge around my father."

She hums again, and the pen continues to scratch as she presumably takes notes on my dramatic response to all this. "Emerson, have you been in therapy before?"

I can't help the laugh that slips out as I tell her, "Um, no. That's never been on the table."

"Well, I'm very glad you called and chose to start now. I want to ensure you understand that you deserve to feel safe and protected, and working in therapy can help you achieve that." My breath comes rapidly, and I sit on the floor, absorbing Zara's words. "You are allowed to be happy, Emerson. Would you like to schedule an appointment and get started?"

In a haze of adrenaline, I tell her I'm wide open during the daytime hours. I locate the insurance card Gunnar left for me and provide Zara with all the information, scheduling an appointment for the next day. I'm stunned by how much better I feel when we hang up the phone.

CHAPTER 32
GUNNAR

My pre-game routine in Minnesota feels different tonight. Not just because we're on the road but because I can hear Emerson's laugh floating down from the family section during warmups. She's up there with Cam and Essence, all three in matching jerseys with their guy's name on the back. This will be her first time watching me play on the road, and I like having her there for me.

It's been a long week with a lot of hard conversations every evening. Emerson invited me to join her for one of her therapy sessions with Zara, where I learned about how people respond after spending their whole lives with parents like Emerson's. I've only met my in-laws once, during that unfortunate time in New York, and I have absolutely no desire to share space with them ever again. I'm afraid I'd throttle them for what they've done to my wife's central nervous system.

Luckily, I'm way on board for Zara's plan to shower Emerson with love and encouragement. If I toss in some really incredible sex, that's just gravy.

I adjust my pads and watch Grentley take his place in

the crease for the first period. The guy's been less of a dick lately. Still won't look me in the eye most days, but at least he's stopped trying to shoulder-check me in the locker room.

My phone buzzes in my stall—a notification that Emerson has posted another photo to her social media. I grin at the image—her between Cam and Essence, all making fish faces at the camera. The caption reads, "Still don't understand icing but loving game day with my PAWs!"

She's gotten good at this, finding the sweet spot between the polished posts Brian wants and genuine moments that show her personality. Way better than those stiff symphony publicity shots her father used to make her do.

"Stag!" Coach barks. "Phone away. Game face on."

I nod and settle in to watch the first period. Something feels off about Grentley's movements. He looks stiff, particularly on his right side. Most people might not notice, but I've been observing his style all season.

Between periods, I find him in the hallway outside the locker room, grimacing as he stretches his hip. St. Paul is ahead by one, and everyone feels tense.

"You good?" I keep my voice neutral, remembering how I felt watching my brother Odin work through recovery from injury.

Grentley's head snaps up. "Fine." But he winces as he straightens.

"Look," I say as I lean against the wall, giving him space. "My brother ended his career with an injury. I've seen how that can wreck a guy. Just... be smart about it."

He stares at me for a long moment. "You angling for my spot, rookie?"

"I'm trying to have your back." I meet his eyes. "We're on the same team."

Coach rounds the corner before Grentley can respond. Takes one look at him and jerks his chin at me. "Warm up, Stag. You're in for the third."

I expect Grentley to argue, but he just nods and heads for the trainer's room. Progress.

The third period flies by in that hyper-focused way that only happens when I'm truly in the zone. Every save feels instinctive, my body moving before my brain can catch up. When the final horn sounds, signaling our 3-1 victory, I'm swarmed by teammates.

"Nice work, G Stag!" Tucker pounds my back while Alder tries to dump water on my head.

I scan the crowd and find Emerson leaning against the glass, beaming. She's holding her phone, probably documenting the celebration for Brian's PR strategy, but her smile is meant just for me. God, I love her. I really need to *tell* her that. I keep meaning to say it, but I'm worried I'll overwhelm her and drive her away. I've been trying to show her as much as I can.

In the locker room, Grentley's waiting by my stall. "Good game," he says gruffly.

"Thanks." I start unbuckling my pads. "You let them check out that hip?"

He sighs. "Yeah. Probably just tweaked it." He pauses. "Listen, about all the shit earlier this season..."

"Water under the bridge." I hold out my fist, and he bumps it. "We're good."

The media scrum descends, asking about the win, about splitting time with Grentley, and about finding my groove as a rookie. I give them the usual soundbites about teamwork and taking it one game at a time. But when someone asks about Emerson being at the game, I can't help but grin.

"Yeah, she's up there with the other PAWs. Still claims she doesn't understand sports, but she's getting into it."

"Any truth to the rumors about tension between you and Ashley Weber?"

My stomach clenches, but I keep my voice steady. "Ashley's a colleague and friend. We're both focused on growing the game, especially supporting the women's league."

"But the tabloids—"

"Are tabloids." I cut them off firmly. "My wife and I are very happy. Now, any questions about tonight's game?"

Later, after showering and changing, I find Emerson waiting in the hall. She's still wearing my jersey, her curls wild from celebrating. "Nice saves out there, husband."

I pull her close, breathing in her familiar scent of lavender and chamomile. "Nice work up there cheering, wife."

She laughs against my chest. "I'm getting better at it, and I posted pictures online. Essence showed me these filters that make everyone look like they're glowing." She pulls back to look at me. "Everything okay? That reporter's question about Ashley pissed me off."

"Brian's handling it, and good for you for naming your emotion about it." I kiss her forehead. "You ready to head back to the hotel?"

"Mm." She leans into me. "Cam and Essence want to grab food first. You up for it?"

"Always." I grab her hand as we head for the exit. My phone buzzes—probably Brian with more PR strategies or coach wanting to review the film. But right now, I just want to enjoy dinner with my wife and our friends, feeling settled in my game and in us.

The headline alert that flashes across my screen stops me cold: "FURY STAR'S VEGAS WEDDING VALIDITY QUESTIONED"

Emerson squeezes my hand. "What's wrong?"

I force a smile and delete the news app from my phone. "Nothing important. Let's get food." But my gut churns, wondering what fresh hell is about to rain down on us just when things are growing solid.

I'll check the full story later and figure out what we're dealing with. For now, I just want to hold onto this moment— my wife proud of my game, our friends waiting, and the team working together. Whatever's coming, we'll face it like we face everything else. Together.

CHAPTER 33
GUNNAR

"Turn left at Bigelow," Emerson says from the passenger seat, checking the map on her new phone...one that her family can't access to traumatize her with their abusive bullshit.

"You got it, Salty." I grin as I merge onto the road leading to the public ice rink. It's been a pretty good week, all things considered. She ramped up therapy and promised not to run away from our marriage without discussing things first. I reassured her that she is not threatening my career, and I'm not going anywhere ... except to away hockey games. I hate leaving her, but she's got her thing going with those music kids.

And now we're going to cuddle cute dogs. Best day ever.

My phone chimes through the car speakers. "Call from...Ashley Weber and Jack Thompson," the system announces.

I grin and glance at Emerson before accepting. "Ready?" She nods, and I click the green icon.

"Hey, guys," Ashley's voice fills the car. "Thanks for chatting. I know you have an event today."

"We appreciate you both being willing to address this head-on," Thompson adds.

"Absolutely." I squeeze Emerson's knee. Thompson and Ashley are also sick of the press asking invasive questions they wouldn't dream of asking if I were swapping shop talk with him instead. "Brian says the joint statement is ready to go live when we give the word, and we've got social media posts in the hopper."

"Right on," Ashley says. "The shelters here in Boston and Pittsburgh are going to receive a lot of attention." I hear a dog yip in the background during the call. "Silver lining, right?"

Emerson smiles. "I think some of the kids from Scale Up are going to show up today, too. Though I did explain we have a no-dogs rule at music lessons."

Everyone laughs, and I feel pride swelling in my chest. My wife has fully embraced Brian's plan of going absolutely public with our joy. She and Ashley have been texting and get along wonderfully. I'm not going to say Thompson is my best friend—he's a rival goalie, after all—but he and I both have a vested interest in making nice. It's a good thing all four of us are dog lovers.

I listen as Emerson talks shop with Ashley—not about hockey strategy but the realities of being a hockey player, such as identifying a social media brand. My wife navigates all of this as if she were born for the game, not like someone whose father is trying to destroy her life.

We finalize the timing details as Emerson guides me to the parking lot of the city ice rink. Through the glass surrounding the outdoor rink, I can see the carpet they've laid over one end of the ice, creating a space for the shelter dogs. However, nobody explained that to the dogs, who are sliding all over the place with their tongues out and eyes bright.

"Good luck today, guys," Thompson says. "And Gun, nice shutout against St. Paul, man."

"Ha. Thanks. See your ass next week in Boston."

After we hang up, I squeeze Emerson's hand. "You okay? Ready?"

She nods. "Talking to Zara helps so much. So does the new phone number." She grins. "Although your mom texts more than my parents ever did."

"Yeah, well, there are a lot of us Stags to wrangle," Emerson laughs. We've been trying to pinpoint a date for our annual Stagsgiving feast. Since so many of us play professional sports, we can never celebrate holidays on the actual day. Mom finally secured a ten-hour block when all 25 of us can make it to the mountain vacation house, even if it means sticking Odin and Wyatt on a red-eye flight back to London after dinner.

Emerson furrows her brow as she glances at the latest text thread regarding sleeping arrangements. "Is there truly enough space for all of us? For an entire weekend?"

"Always room for family, Salty." I kiss her cheek. "Let's go pet some puppies."

She smiles and tucks her phone into her leggings. I watch her get out of the car rather than run around and open her door, just this once. I want to admire her backside in the leggings. She's wearing a Stag jersey, obviously, and the combination of my name on her back and those tight pants … I need to remember that we've got dogs waiting for us. Sexy thoughts about my wife's curves will have to wait.

The scene at the ice rink is controlled chaos. At least thirty dogs of various sizes romp on the ice while my teammates crouch and crawl among them, wearing jeans, skates, and jerseys. The twins lie on their backs on the ice, covered in pit bulls. Behind the boards, dozens of phones record the mayhem while Brian directs photographers to "get the wholesome shots."

Seeing me and Emerson arrive, Brian waves. "Ten minutes until we open to the public," he announces. Then turns back to the press. "Take lots of pictures. I don't want any questions about the validity of this puppy love."

Brian's use of the word 'validity' lands like a slapshot. I remember that I deleted the news app from my phone after I saw something that people—probably Emerson's parents—are saying our marriage isn't real. I have got to stop acting without thinking, and I know I need to talk to Brian about this, but just as I decide, a shelter volunteer releases the hounds.

I drop to my knees, still wearing sneakers, and am immediately swarmed by a group of mutts. A golden retriever mix plants her paws on my shoulders and licks my entire face while some sort of terrier yaps at me, chewing my shoelaces.

"The internet is going to love you," Emerson laughs as she records on her phone. I bite back my response about me loving her because we haven't had that conversation yet. I don't know why I keep stalling on that. I don't want to overwhelm her while she's working on freeing herself from her father's influence. A big lick right on my eyeball pulls me from those thoughts.

"Take a pic of me," I manage to say between face-washings. "Then come get your own puppy therapy."

Even Grentley seems to enjoy himself, actually smiling as he tosses a puck for a border collie to chase across the carpet. The dog brings it back to him every time, tail wagging furiously.

"That's quite the save percentage," I hear Coach remark, and Grentley actually laughs. I resist the urge to make a fart sound at him.

While I give belly scratches and nose rubs, I notice Cam, Essence, and Emerson huddled near the boards, checking their phones. Banksy slides across the ice near me, and the dog on his chest swaps places with the one on my face. Cam yells, "Our lease definitely allows pets, babe."

"Same!" Essence sighs, seeming less enthused.

Banksy and Cappy look at one another, and both dive for the golden, trying to lay claim on the friendliest dog out there.

I notice Alder looking cozy with a chunky boy draped across his lap. "I'm in love," he announces. "Look at this face." The dog immediately rolls to face me, tongue lolling.

"That dog is cross-eyed," I observe.

Tucker squeals. "You're getting him, right?"

Alder beams and ruffles the dog's ears. "Already texted the landlord, bro. His new name is Gordon."

The next hour is a blur of photos, autographs, and interviews. Brian orchestrates everything perfectly—players with puppies, kids meeting their heroes, and shelter staff explaining the adoption processes. Emerson even brings some of her music kiddos around and shows them how to pet the dogs, and I catch her chatting with the shelter staff about kids playing music for the pups to help socialize the dogs while the kids practice for their upcoming concert.

A reporter pauses and asks Emerson if she and I will be adopting today, and she smiles. "We're still settling into our routine at home," she explains diplomatically. "But we're so excited to be Aunt and Uncle to Alder's boy, Gordie."

By the time the animal folks declare that the pups need to return, I'm a strange combination of exhaustion, delight, and energy. Above all, I'm eager to get home and shower with my wife.

CHAPTER 34
EMERSON

Steam fills the bathroom as I run my fingers through Gunnar's beard, feeling each coarse hair against my fingertips. "Getting scruffy," I murmur, tracing his jaw. Water droplets cling to the golden strands, and I'm struck by how different he looks from the clean-cut athlete in his milk commercial.

"Can't shave during a win streak." He presses me against the cool tile, his calloused hands sliding down my sides, leaving trails of heat in their wake. "Bad luck."

"Mmm. Very superstitious." I love these quiet moments- just us, no drama. Our apartment has become a haven for us in the past few weeks. I know I need to confront my family eventually, that I can't hide behind a changed phone number forever. But for now, I have exactly what I need. I officially moved into Gunnar's bedroom …our bedroom. I also transferred all my stuff into this bathroom, and I enjoy seeing the shelves with both our products blended together. United.

Zara has been very encouraging in helping me notice these small pleasures. We've been meeting twice a week, partly because I have the time and partly because she believes I can benefit from a lot from practical skills, such as setting boundaries. I haven't spoken to my parents or any symphony personnel in weeks, which feels great.

And I'm learning to lower my boundaries with Gunnar, which feels even better. He's been so amazing, sitting with me for therapy sessions and taking notes. He jokes that physical intimacy is the only homework assignment he's ever enjoyed. And my goodness, am I learning to love physical intimacy. I don't know if my body was waiting for Gunnar or if he just sets me free from whatever pressures were bottling up my sex drive, but I'm ravenous for his body and the things it can do with mine.

The shower feels warm and comforting as Gunnar's hands cup my backside, and I gasp, arching into him. Our wet skin slides together, creating delicious friction. "Careful. I'm still tender from this morning."

He grins, that cocky smile that first drew me to him in Vegas. "You weren't complaining then."

"Never." I stretch up to kiss him, savoring his taste and touch. Everything about him feels like home—the solid warmth of his chest against mine, the gentle way he holds me despite his tremendous strength, the familiar scent of his soap mixing with the steam. I feel safe here, protected, and loved.

"God, I love you." The words slip out before I can catch them, carried on a wave of pure emotion.

Gunnar freezes, water running in rivulets down his face. For a terrifying moment, I worry I've ruined everything. Then his face breaks into the most brilliant smile I've ever seen, brighter than after any shutout victory.

"Say it again, Salty."

My heart swells. "I love you."

He lifts me, pressing me harder against the wall. I love how he can haul me around despite my substantial weight. His beard scratches my neck, and his erection digs into my stomach as he whispers, "I love you too, Salty. So fucking much."

The kiss deepens, his hands everywhere at once. "I've wanted to tell you for weeks," he groans.

"Me, too," I pant, wrapping my legs around his waist, not caring about being sore anymore. This man, my husband, loves me—really loves me—not because of my family name or my musical talent or what I can do for his career. He loves *me*.

Breaking the kiss, Gunnar traces patterns on my skin in the shower. His touch is reverent, like I'm something precious. "Why didn't you?"

He pinches my nipple, and I gasp. "Why didn't you?" I lower a hand to his cock and squeeze, loving the sound this draws from his throat.

"Didn't want to overwhelm you. With everything happening with your father..."

I silence him with a kiss. "You're nothing like him. You make me feel safe. Loved." I slide my mouth wherever I can reach. "Protected but not controlled. Supported but not stifled. Free to be myself." I pull back and meet his eye. "Also, I don't want to talk about my father right now."

Gunnar laughs against my lips, hoisting me just a wee bit higher against the wall and I feel the blunt head of his cock pressing against my entrance. "You ready, baby? You want this?"

I nod. "Please." The shower head is big enough with enough water pressure that neither of us is outside the warm spray. That, combined with the heat lamp in the bathroom, means the whole space is warm and slippery.

Gunnar, soaped and rinsed and smelling amazing, licks the length of my throat as he eases inside my body, and every bit of me sighs at the welcome pressure. "Oh, I am so full, Gunny. Thank you."

My head falls back against the shower wall as he starts to move. I cling to him as his hands dig into the flesh of my thighs while he utters filthy, appreciative words about my body.

"Look at those legs spread just for me, Emerson. Fuck, I'm so deep inside you. I feel every soft inch of your skin everywhere, baby. So wet and warm for me. Fucckkkkk."

My skin hums with the need to release. After the day we spent together watching him crawl around the ice with rescued dogs and city kids who love his team, I've been desperate for this. I start to wriggle in his arms, rubbing my nipples along his chest, moaning at the friction. My nails dig into his tattooed flesh as he thrusts, grunting. It's filthy and perfect and everything I never dared to want.

Being with Gunnar has let me become myself. "I love you," I pant, tilting my hips until my clit is pressed against his pubic bone. "I love you so much, Gunny."

I don't mean to use a pet name for him, but it just feels right as my body starts pulsing. He beams at my words and reaction. "Oh shit, baby, I feel you starting to come. You like that?" I nod, biting my lip, so close I can see stars. "Yeah, take what you need, wife. Grind against me. I'm going to fill you up after you come. Fuck, Emerson. Fuck!"

I squeeze my legs around his waist, my belly jiggling with his thrusts, coming so hard I worry the waves will make him drop me. But I know he's got me, keeping me safe. Gunnar presses his forehead against mine and bellows my name, a desperate shout as he pulses inside me, the warmth of his release as precious as the sound of him repeating that he loves me.

After, he lowers me to the floor, breathing heavily. "Salty, that was incredible. It's never been this good for me."

I smile, lazily running my fingers through his wet, shaggy hair. "Well, you know it's never been good for me before you."

He kisses my hand. "You just needed me to find you."

"That's more true than you know, Gunnar." He kisses me, long and sweet, and reaches behind me to shut off the water. Someday, maybe I'll care about our astronomical water bill, but for now, I just want to revel in the sensation of my giant husband patting me dry with a fluffy towel, tying a matching one around his waist.

"I can't wait to lie in bed beside you again." His grin is contagious. I don't know if it's normal to feel drunk after sex, but it's certainly a common occurrence for me. I hum as I pad into our bedroom, still naked but with a towel around my hair.

I slide under the covers that smell like him, like us, and I smile, thinking of all our mornings and nights ahead in this room. A thud at the door interrupts my thoughts, and Gunnar pulls on his sweats to go investigate.

He pads back into the room, holding an envelope and wearing a puzzled expression as he climbs into bed beside me. "Did you know this was delivered? It was shoved under the door."

I shake my head and burrow against his side. The envelope is addressed to me, and I open it to reveal crisp white paper with an embossed letterhead from Weintraub, Stein and Associates, LLP. My stomach drops at the sight of my family's attorney. "Should we read it together or pass it back and forth like old people with a newspaper?" I try to joke, but my voice trembles.

He huffs. "I don't like the look of this." I trace my finger along the seal, hesitating. Taking a deep breath, I begin to read aloud. My hands start to tremble, and my voice falters after the salutation.

"What is it?" Gunnar asks, leaning closer.

"It's... it's from my parents' lawyers." I swallow hard. "They're... they're filing for a conservatorship over me."

"A what?" Gunnar sits up straighter, all traces of post-intimacy relaxation gone.

"They're trying to be my guardians, like Britney Spears' parents." I continue reading, my voice growing tighter with each sentence. "They're claiming I'm 'mentally unstable' and 'unable to make appropriate decisions for my own well-being.' That I'm 'delusional' and... and that I 'believe myself to be married when no valid marriage exists.'"

Gunnar's face darkens. "Son of a bitch. I totally forgot that fucking headline." He starts to yank on his hair.

I turn to face him. "What do you mean?"

He swallows and tells me he received an alert back in New York that "sources" suggested our marriage was invalid. "And then I fucking forgot about it, and things were going so great, baby. I just thought it was gossip."

I blink at him. "The letter states that I've exhibited 'erratic behavior,' including 'abandoning a prestigious career for unsubstantiated claims of mistreatment.'" My voice falters. "That I require a guardian to protect me from further self-destructive choices."

"Holy shit, Emerson." Gunnar's jaw clenches. "This is about control. They can't stand that you're building your own life."

As the words sink in, my mind races with terrifying possibilities. Could they truly do this? Force me back to New York? Place me under their legal control?

Gunnar rubs his temples. "Damn it, I should have called Brian right away."

I stare at the letter, trying to keep my breathing steady. "They say that because our marriage wasn't legal, it's evidence I'm not thinking clearly. That I've been 'manipulated' and need protection."

"We were there. We're married, Emerson." He spins the silicone band on his finger. "Maybe not legally yet, but we will be."

"You don't understand." Fear grips my chest. "If they succeed with this, I won't have any control. They'll dictate everything – where I live, my finances, my medical decisions. They could force me into treatment I don't need nor want."

Gunnar's eyes flash with determination. He reaches for his phone. "I'm calling Tim right now. Your parents aren't the only ones with lawyers."

I grab his wrist. "Gunnar, I can't fight them. They have connections, resources—"

"Hey." He cradles my face between his hands. "Look at me. You are not alone in this. The Stags fight like wolves for our own, remember? And you're one of us now."

His intensity steadies me slightly. "But what if—"

"No 'what ifs.' We're going to fix this, Emerson," he says, pressing his forehead to mine. "I promise."

"How?" I whisper, the letter still clutched in my trembling hand.

"First, we call Uncle Tim. Next, we make our marriage official, iron-clad, witnessed by a hundred people if necessary." His thumb brushes away a tear I didn't know had fallen. "And then we show your parents – and anyone else who's watching – that you are exactly where you want to be."

I close my eyes, drawing strength from his certainty. "I love you," I tell him, the words feeling less like a declaration and more like a lifeline.

"I love you too, Salty." He pulls me closer, his heartbeat steady against my ear. "We've got this. Together."

I believe in him. For the first time in my life, I genuinely feel that I'm not facing my battles alone.

CHAPTER 35
EMERSON

"I keep thinking about running." I trace the pattern on Zara's couch with my finger, the conservatorship letter weighing heavily in my bag. "It would be easier for everyone."

"Everyone, you mean Gunnar?" Zara's voice is gentle yet firm.

"If I'm not here, my parents have no case. They'd leave him alone." I twist my silicone wedding band. "His career wouldn't be impacted by this legal circus."

"Is that what Gunnar wants?"

I gaze out of her office window at the Pittsburgh skyline. "He says no, but he doesn't fully understand what my parents are capable of."

"Based on what you've shared, your parents are employing legal measures to try to regain control over you." Zara puts her notepad down. "Running away would actually reinforce their claim that you're unstable and making irrational choices."

The truth of her words settles like a stone in my stomach. "So they win either way."

"Not necessarily," Zara leans forward. "Emerson, I want you to know that I'd be more than willing to testify regarding your mental stability and capacity. In my professional assessment, you're completely capable of making your own decisions."

I blink back unexpected tears. "You would do that?"

"Of course. You're in therapy not because you're unstable, but because you're working through the effects of controlling relationships and discovering your autonomy. That demonstrates remarkable self-awareness and mental clarity."

"My father will bring in psychiatrists who've never even met me."

"And they'll have far less credibility than someone who's been working with you regularly." She smiles reassuringly. "The courts typically favor the testimony of treating professionals over that of hired experts."

A tendril of hope uncurls within me. "Tim—Gunnar's uncle—says the same thing."

"Your support network is strong, Emerson, and that's another point in your favor. Individuals who need conservatorships typically lack support systems. You have Gunnar, his family, your colleagues at Scale Up, and even your students."

I hadn't thought of it that way. "So, you don't think they'll succeed?"

"Cases like this require substantial evidence of incapacity. Based on everything you've shared, you're functioning exceptionally well." She glances at her watch. "We're almost out of time, but I want you to take something with you today."

She writes on her prescription pad and hands it to me. I

read the words: *Emerson Saltzer demonstrates sound judgment and complete capacity to make her own decisions.*

"My official assessment. Keep it with you until we need it formally."

I fold the paper carefully. "Thank you."

"One more thing." Zara smiles. "Next time you feel the urge to run, remember that standing your ground is the strongest move you can make right now."

As I step into the elevator, my phone buzzes with a text from Gunnar:

> Practice done. Want to get lunch before meeting with Tim?

I answer immediately:

> Yes please. I have news from Zara.

His response warms me:

> Proud of you, Salty. See you at Mel's in 20. Love you.

I press the phone to my chest, drawing strength from his words. Running isn't the answer. Fighting is.

I arrive at our favorite diner before Gunnar and claim our usual booth in the back corner. The owner, Mel, slides a chocolate shake in front of me without asking.

"You look like you could use this today, honey."

I smile gratefully. "That obvious, huh?"

"Nothing, a little sugar can't help." She pats my hand. "Your man just pulled up."

Gunnar enters shortly after, his hair still damp from his post-practice shower. Despite everything, my heart still flutters at the sight of him. He slides into the seat opposite me, immediately reaching for my hands across the table.

"How was Zara?"

"Surprisingly helpful." I pull out the note she gave me. "She's willing to testify about my mental competence."

He reads it, his face brightening. "This is huge, Salty."

"She says it'll carry more weight than any 'expert' my father brings in."

"Tim will be thrilled. He's assembling our entire strategy right now." Gunnar squeezes my hands. "We meet with the full legal team at three. Mom asked me to reassure you that she's worked in family law her whole career and knows influential people high up."

Mel brings Gunnar's usual burger and sets my fries down without interrupting our conversation. I take a small bite, surprised to feel my appetite returning.

"What did Brian say about the publicity angle?" I ask.

"He's drafting a statement denouncing your parents' actions as retaliatory for the symphony investigation." Gunnar dips a fry in ketchup. "Says we'll have public opinion solidly on our side."

"But what about your endorsements? The hospital?"

"Already taken care of. I spoke directly with their board members. It turns out that several of them have had experiences with controlling family members." He smiles grimly. "Rich people problems, I suppose."

I stir my shake, processing all this. "I can't believe how quickly everyone has mobilized."

"Family takes care of family." He says it so matter-of-factly, as if it's the most natural thing in the world. For him, it is.

"I'm still scared," I admit quietly.

"I'd be worried if you weren't. But Emerson—" he

catches my gaze, his blue eyes intense, "—we are going to win this. Your parents have money and connections, but we have the truth and some pretty decent connections of our own."

I draw a deep breath. "Zara says running would only prove their point."

"Smart woman, that Zara." He winks, lightening the moment. "Almost as smart as my wife."

I manage a small smile. "What should I expect at this meeting?"

"Tim is bringing his two best associates, along with a family law specialist who deals with conservatorship cases." Gunnar checks his watch. "We should head out soon. Tim wants us to review some documents before the full team arrives."

I hesitate, as something that's been bothering me finally surfaces. "Gunnar, I noticed you didn't start the last two games. Is that because of all this?" I gesture vaguely, encompassing the legal mess we're in. "The rotation schedule changed."

He sighs, running a hand through his damp hair. "Coach thought it might be better if I focused on this for a bit."

"I knew it." My chest tightens with guilt. "You're losing ice time because of me and my family drama."

"Hey, look at me." He cups my face gently. "I'm okay riding the bench for a few games while we get this sorted. Grentley's playing well, and the team is winning."

"But your career—"

"It will be fine," he interrupts firmly. "We've got years ahead of us, Salty. A few games now don't define anything. What matters is ensuring that your parents can't control your life anymore."

"You're sure?"

His smile is genuine. "Positive. Besides, Coach says the rest might be good for me. Keep me hungry." He winks. "And trust me, I'm very hungry to get back out there and show everyone what I can do." As we walk to his car, I feel something shifting inside me—fear is giving way to determination. My parents thought this legal threat would break me and send me crawling back to them. Instead, it's only strengthening my resolve.

CHAPTER 36
GUNNAR

I ADJUST MY TIE AS WE ENTER UNCLE TIM'S LAW OFFICE, Emerson's hand firmly clasped in mine. The entire floor exudes money and power –polished wood and glass complementing views of the three rivers converging. Tim's domain. And today, our war room.

Emerson looks small beside the massive conference table, but her spine is straight as she arranges her notes. I've never been prouder of her. Three weeks ago, she might have run from this fight. Now, she's preparing for battle.

"Sorry we're late," Mom announces, sweeping into the room in her pantsuit, briefcase in hand. "Docket ran long."

I wasn't expecting her, but I'm not surprised. The Stags mobilize for family.

"Juniper." Emerson's face brightens. "You didn't have to come."

Mom squeezes her shoulder. "Of course I did. Besides, I've dealt with family court judges for over twenty years. I might as well put that knowledge to use. Besides," she rolls her eyes, "Tim's focus is sports law. He needs me, whether he'll admit it or not."

Uncle Tim enters with three associates trailing behind him. His usual scowl deepens as he tosses a folder onto the table. "These Saltzer people are something else."

"Tell me about it," I mutter, pulling out Emerson's chair.

Uncle Tim slaps the table. "I've reviewed the conservatorship filing. It's aggressive but deeply flawed."

Emerson's fingers tighten around mine. "So, they actually filed it?"

"Yesterday in New York," Tim confirms as he takes his seat. "But we've already filed a motion to dismiss along with a counter-petition for harassment and defamation."

Mom leans forward. "The jurisdiction itself poses a problem for them. You have established residence in Pennsylvania."

"They claim I'm only here temporarily," Emerson says quietly. "That I was...taken advantage of during a mental health crisis."

My jaw tightens. "That's bullshit."

"Of course it is," Mom agrees smoothly. "Which is why we've gathered substantial evidence of your independence and capacity."

Tim's associate distributes thick folders to each of us. I open mine to discover affidavits from Scale Up, testimonials from Emerson's students, and a note from Emerson's therapist.

"We also have documented evidence of your father's controlling behavior and retaliation," Tim adds.

"The symphony board is cooperating fully," Mom notes. "With us. Not him."

I squeeze Emerson's hand under the table as she emits a low, shocked sound. "See? We've got this."

Tim adjusts his glasses. "There's something else you should know." His expression softens – a rare sight. "Your father's position with the symphony is becoming increasingly precarious. The administrative leave may become permanent."

Emerson blinks. "What does that mean for their case?"

"It means they likely don't have the resources for a prolonged legal battle," Mom explains. "Conservatorship cases are expensive, especially when contested."

I lean back, processing this. "So you're saying they're bluffing?"

"I'm saying they're desperate," Tim corrects. "Which makes them dangerous but also vulnerable."

Mom exchanges a look with Tim. "We think it's time to go on the offensive."

One of the associates who helped prepare my contract with the Fury earlier this year slides a document across the table. "We're proposing a cease and desist with very specific terms. They must drop all proceedings, agree to no contact without your explicit consent, and we won't pursue a harassment suit that would further damage your father's reputation."

I watch Emerson's face as she reads the document. She's been so worried about my career taking hits that she hasn't fully processed what her father stands to lose.

"They won't agree to this," she says finally.

"They will if they're smart," Tim replies. "Your father's future depends on rehabilitating his image. A prolonged legal battle with his 'mentally unstable' daughter won't help that cause."

I shift in my seat. "What about our marriage? They're using the Vegas thing against us."

"Already handled," Mom smiles. "I've arranged for Judge Hernandez to officiate a legal ceremony next week. Unless you'd like me to do it."

"You can do that?" Emerson asks.

Mom winks. "There are advantages to twenty years on the bench, dear."

I feel the knot in my chest loosen for the first time since the letter arrived. We have a plan, we have power, and we have family.

"What do we do now?" I ask.

"First," Tim says, checking his watch, "we have that video conference call with the Saltzers and their counsel in five minutes." My stomach tightens. Tim nods to an assistant hovering in the doorway. "Set up the zoom machine."

As the large screen on the wall flickers to life, I try not to laugh at my Uncle's attempt at a technology joke. I move closer to Emerson, watching her gather herself. She straightens her shoulders and lifts her chin—little movements transforming her from the woman who once flinched at confrontation to someone ready for battle.

"You don't have to say anything," I whisper. "Tim and Mom can handle this."

Emerson shakes her head. "No. I need to speak for myself. That's the whole point."

The screen splits to reveal Emerson's parents and their lawyer in a sterile white conference room in New York. The contrast between our spaces couldn't be more stark. Her mother's pearls gleam against her silk blouse, while her father's face is already reddening above his perfectly knotted tie.

"Emerson." Her mother's voice is clipped. "You look... healthy."

I almost snort at the passive-aggressive dig but keep my face neutral. This is Emerson's moment.

"I am healthy," she responds evenly. "And happy."

Her father scoffs. "Happy? Playing nursery tunes with street children? That's hardly a productive use of your talents."

I feel my fists clench beneath the table. The smug condescension in his voice makes me want to put my fist through the screen.

"Those children deserve music education," Emerson says, her voice steady. "And I deserve to teach how I choose."

"You deserve nothing." Her father's fist hits the table. "We gave you everything—the best teachers, the finest opportunities. And you threw it all away for what? Some hockey thug and his uncouth family?"

I tense but keep silent. Tim shoots me a warning glance. This isn't about me.

"You gave me restrictions. Expectations. Control." Emerson's words flow with surprising strength. "But the Stags gave me something better—they gave me choice."

"Choice?" Her mother's laugh is brittle. "You chose to embarrass us. To destroy your father's reputation with these ridiculous allegations—"

"The allegations," Tim interrupts smoothly, "are well-documented. Would you like to review the testimony from female musicians? The pattern of discrimination? The hostile work environment?"

Their lawyer, a rail-thin man with wire-rimmed glasses, shifts uncomfortably. "Perhaps we should discuss terms."

"Terms?" Her father's face purples. "There are no terms. She will return to New York, resume her proper place—"

"That's not happening." Emerson's voice rings clear and strong. I've never heard her sound so certain. "I'm not your puppet anymore."

"You ungrateful—" Her father starts to rise, but their lawyer grabs his arm.

"Mr. Saltzer," the lawyer's tone is sharp. "That's enough." He turns to the camera. "My clients need to change strategy. The board's investigation is conclusive. Fighting this will only cause further damage."

Her mother's face crumples. "What are you saying?"

"I'm saying it's done." The lawyer shuffles papers. "The best course now is to accept the administrative leave and focus on damage control."

Her father slumps in his chair, defeat etched into every line of his face. It's an expression I've never seen before on the rare occasions I've encountered him—the great maestro, finally conducting his last performance.

"So, this is how you end our relationship." Her mother's voice breaks. "After everything we've done for you."

"No." Emerson leans forward, and I place my hand on her back, feeling her strength. "This is how I begin my own life. Without your control, without your criticism, without your constant disapproval."

"You're nothing without us," her father spits. "Nothing."

Mom stiffens beside me, but Emerson doesn't flinch.

"I'm everything without you," she tells them. "I'm a musician who brings joy instead of pressure. I'm a teacher who builds confidence instead of fear. I'm a wife who is truly loved." She takes a deep breath. "I'm finally myself."

Tim moves to end the call, but I can't resist leaning forward into frame.

"This isn't the end," I say, looking directly at her father. "It's just the beginning of the Emerson Era."

The screen goes dark. In the silence that follows, I pull Emerson close and kiss her temple.

"You okay?" I ask softly.

She nods, a smile spreading across her face. "Better than okay."

Uncle Tim's associate starts gathering her papers. "Well, that was productive. I'll file the cease and desist regarding the mental health allegations immediately. They won't risk any further legal exposure."

Tim looks impressed—a rare expression for him. "Well done, Emerson. I think we've seen the last of their legal maneuvers."

Mom squeezes Emerson's shoulder. "I'm proud of you, sweetheart."

As we prepare to leave, Emerson turns to me. "Did you mean what you said? About this being the beginning?"

I cup her face in my hands. "Every word. The beginning of our real life together. No more pretending, no more doubts."

"No more running," she adds.

"Exactly." I grin. "Now, how about we grab the twins and get some victory pierogies?"

"God, yes." She laughs, and the sound fills me with more satisfaction than any shutout I've ever achieved. "I love you, you know that?"

"I had a pretty good idea." I take her hand as we head toward the door. "But I love hearing it."

CHAPTER 37
GUNNAR

Scanning the packed house, I adjust my tie in the Scale Up auditorium. Emerson has no idea that I pulled out my Armani for tonight. She left long before I got dressed. The twins and half the Fury team fill two rows, all of us in suits that would fit in the world's finest symphony. Hell, these kids deserve the effort.

Even Grentley showed up, though he's sitting apart from us. After we dealt with our legal shit, my game improved a lot and Coach has me and Grentley back on a regular rotation. Grentley doesn't love it, but he doesn't actively hate me, either.

Everyone clutches elaborate bouquets for the performers - Coach's idea, surprisingly. He said if we're going to support youth music, we're doing it right.

Parents whisper and point at the hockey players, but the kids walking onto the stage only have eyes for their instruments. That's what I love about this place—it's all about the music.

The program in my hands lists "Emerson Saltzer - Strings Instructor," causing my chest to swell with pride.

She resisted accepting the job offer last week, concerned that her father's influence might extend even here. However, Scale Up doesn't care about symphony politics and family drama. They just care that she loves music and kids. Now, my wife proudly serves as a part-time teacher at this organization, and I've never been more excited to buy anyone business cards. In fact, I've never purchased business cards for anyone else, and my excitement led me to rush and misspell "instructor." Emerson loves them anyway.

She needs small wins. She's pretty fragile after discovering her father was placed on "administrative leave." The symphony board's investigation confirmed everything - the hostile environment, the gender discrimination, the controlling behavior. Emerson carries a lot of guilt about it, worrying about her parents' finances, their reputation. But Zara is helping her understand that her father created these consequences for himself. As her therapist says, "not your sewer, not your rats." Emerson will get there. I'll help her.

The lights dim, and the first group takes the stage - beginning violin students sawing enthusiastically through "Hot Cross Buns." We cheer as if they just scored a hat trick. Tucker actually tears up when a nervous student rushes off stage in tears, then comes back with Emerson's guidance and nails her solo. Alder elbows his twin, but I notice him wiping his eyes too.

I watch Emerson in her element between numbers, adjusting stands and whispering encouragement. She's radiant in a black dress that emphasizes her curves rather than hiding them. No more trying to disappear. A far cry from the woman who stepped off that train from New York, terrified but determined.

The cello ensemble brings down the house with their rock medley—Emerson's arrangement. She worked on it for weeks, wanting to show the kids that classical instruments can play any style. Alder whoops so loud that people initially stare at him, but then the crowd starts whooping, too.

Brian sits behind us, probably calculating PR angles, but even he seems genuinely moved. The hospital board meeting went well last week - turns out sick kids don't care about marriage licenses, they just like that I visit. Once Emerson and I went on record explaining that we didn't know the marriage wasn't official and that we intend to fix that as soon as possible, people stopped acting like we were trying to deceive someone. I'm still a "family friendly" athlete worthy of a milk mustache. The endorsements are secure. Not that it matters compared to this - watching my wife help these kids find their voices.

After the final bow, we all surge forward with our flowers. Kids and parents swarm the hockey players - Essence is already organizing a group photo for social media - but I only have eyes for my wife, who's wiping happy tears as she hugs her students.

"That was amazing," I tell her, passing over a massive bouquet of sunflowers - her favorite, I discovered. I love learning new shit about my wife.

"I can't believe they did it." She beams. "Did you hear Jamie's solo? He was so nervous..."

"Mrs. Stag?" A woman with purple hair approaches, accompanied by two guys with man-buns. My wife freezes, recognition flooding her face. She's asked me to stop correcting people who call her that, so I bite my tongue.

"I'm Sarah, from String Fury. This is Mike and Dave."

The woman grins. "We heard your arrangement of the medley. Omar sent us the recording. You've got serious composition skills."

Emerson's eyes go wide. I squeeze her hand as Sarah continues, "We do a lot of educational outreach and workshops with kids. Would you be interested in collaborating? Maybe sit in on some shows?"

"I... yes!" Emerson clutches my arm. "I'd love that."

I kiss her temple as they exchange information, watching her practically vibrate with excitement. My wife is living her dreams her way, no longer hiding who she is or what she wants.

"Ready to go home?" I ask when she's done. The team's organizing a celebration outing, and knowing my brothers, it'll go late.

She looks around at the crowded auditorium—her students proudly showing off their flowers, their found family celebrating alongside them, and her new colleagues already planning future projects. This stands in stark contrast to the sterile symphony halls of her upbringing.

"Actually," she says, "I think I am home."

I pull her close, breathing in the scent of her hair. When my season ends, we'll have another wedding - this time surrounded by everyone who loves us. But watching her now, I realize we never needed papers to prove what we are.

We're partners. We're family.

We're exactly where we're meant to be.

EPILOGUE

GUNNAR: SIX MONTHS LATER

The spring air carries the sounds of laughter as I adjust my bowtie, watching boats drift down the Allegheny. It will be fun to get out there this summer, now that hockey is over.

The second round of playoffs wasn't bad for a rookie season, even if we had to lose to Montreal. Grentley and I made the rotation work – it turns out we're both better goalies when we're not exhausted. But today isn't about hockey.

Today is about forever.

Strands of lights cover our apartment building's riverside patio, and glass bulbs catch the late afternoon light. Simple wooden tables dot the grass in the back, laden with comfort food - my dad's pierogies, Alice's mac and cheese…all the things that make Pittsburgh feel like home. Wildflowers spill from mason jars on the tables, while kayaks from the rec room bob gently at the dock below. Cam has already threatened to throw Banksy in the river if he doesn't dance later.

"Looking good, G Stag." Tucker adjusts my rolled

sleeves, fussing like he hasn't been wearing the exact same outfit all afternoon. "Though I still say jeans at your wedding is a power move."

I grin. "Salty picked them." And the blue bowtie that matches her dress - which I haven't seen yet, but apparently matches my eyes. She fussed about breaking the "no seeing the bride" rule since we're already mentally married, but I wanted to give her this moment. Sure, we signed paperwork at the courthouse. But we both wanted an actual wedding, and I wanted to show Emerson off to my family and friends.

The Scale Up string ensemble tunes up near the water, their small faces serious with concentration. They insisted on playing for their teacher, even though Emerson worried it was asking too much. These kids would do anything for her. Just last week, they performed at the children's hospital - my wife's idea to bridge our worlds. All those kids who are admitted and missing their school performances absolutely loved a change in the routine of their day, even if Emerson says the acoustics are lousy in a hospital.

Tucker finishes adjusting my outfit, and I chase him off to sit with Odin—freshly back from his stint in the UK—and Alder. Alder especially needs a boost after his personal life exploded in the media. I wish I could make it easier for him to be a bisexual pro hockey player, but nobody could have anticipated the blowup at the arena. The twins are still reeling from it, but today isn't meant for dwelling on darkness.

Today is for light, for joy, for choosing each other all over again.

Brian hovers near the bar in - miracle of miracles - actual jeans, probably calculating the PR value of this intimate gathering. But even he tears up when the kids start playing - a sweet, slightly squeaky Canon in D.

"Got the ring, son?" Dad appears at my side to walk me to my place up front.

I nod and smile. "We never actually took the other bands off," I confess. Dad pats my hand. I tilt my head to look at him, fine lines around his eyes from years of smiling. "Do you think it's nuts that I knew Emerson was the one right away?"

He shakes his head. "Nah. It was like that with your mother. One look at her and I knew." He pulls me close and kisses me on the cheek. "You're like me, Gun. We love hard, and we love quick." Dad moves to ruffle my hair, and I duck away from him. "Sorry, kiddo. Don't want to mess up your look for your lady." He clears his throat and walks to his seat beside Mom, who hands him a tissue.

The kids pause in their playing and start the song over again. I look up to the building, waiting for Emerson to emerge—and my heart stops.

She appears in the doorway, radiant in flowing blue silk that clings to her curves before cascading around her legs. Her dark curls are crowned with wildflowers, and her smile outshines the rare Pittsburgh sun. And she's about to be all mine, legally and publicly this time.

The String Fury trio, now Emerson's regular collaborators, begins to play alongside her students. Sarah's purple hair matches the sunset. They have been incredible mentors, demonstrating to Emerson that classical training does not equate to classical limitations.

Mom offered to officiate, but we opted to say brief vows to each other and get to the part where everyone eats. Plus, we wanted her just to be Mom today, crying happy tears between Dad and Tim as Emerson walks toward me. Even her brother Edwin showed up. His dour presence in the back row is an awkward peace offering that means more than he knows.

When Emerson reaches me, I can't help but touch her face. Her skin is warm from the June heat, and her cheeks are flushed with joy. "Hi, Salty." She decided to change her last name to Stag to feel connected to my family. She also says I can call her Salty as much as I want.

"Hi yourself." Her eyes sparkle with mischief and love. "Ready to make this official?"

"Been ready since Vegas."

We speak our vows—simple promises to choose each other every day, fight like wolves for our love, never stop making music together, support dreams and challenge limits, and always, always come home to each other.

Then we exchange rings—metal this time, though we're keeping the silicone ones for game days. Finally, I turn to the crowd and say, "That's it! We're married!" The kids hit a slightly off note, and I pull Emerson in for a somewhat indecent kiss as everyone cheers. Perfect imperfection.

"I love you," Emerson says, a little teary, gazing into my eyes.

"I love you so much." I kiss her forehead. "I can't wait to be with you every day."

She laughs and pokes me with her bouquet. "You already get that, Gunny. It's just more of the same from here on out."

I pull her in for a tight hug. "That sounds amazing."

I hold my wife close. My actual, legal, no-take-backs

wife. She smells like honeysuckle and home. And I get to keep her right here.

As the night goes on, Coach actually dances. Grentley shows up late but brings good whiskey, so all is forgiven.

Emerson's students attempt to teach hockey players the Macarena while String Fury improvises an accompaniment. My wife hands me a fried mushroom from a tray and observes the crowd, smiling. It was crucial to her that everyone felt comfortable. I might have yelled at Brian and threatened to cause another scandal if he didn't dress down.

Emerson sighs. "I still can't believe you got Brian to wear jeans."

I laugh, spinning her under the twinkling lights. As Emerson and I dance and sway, the river catches the last rays of the sunset, painting everything gold. "Anything for you, Salty. Always."

She stretches up to kiss me, soft and sure, and I know - this is what winning really feels like.

Thank you for reading Gunnar and Emerson's love story! My newsletter subscribers get a steamy bonus scene. Visit LaineyDavis.com to subscribe, or scan the QR code below.

Want to know what happened with Alder and his personal life? One-Click Playing for Payback.

AUTHOR'S NOTE

This book has been such a delight for me to write. Ty Stag has always been my favorite Stag, so it makes sense to me that I'm enjoying writing books for his sons. It just feels right for these men to love their heroines so completely.

The world around me feels pretty scary right now, so I needed to escape into the fantasy of this story.

I'm grateful for critiques of early drafts from Elizabeth Perry, Karen Grey, Michelle McCraw, and Ember Leigh. I'm super grateful for hockey authenticity checks from Cathryn Fox, Kelly Jamieson, Val Sweeney, and Dana Rosvanis.

For the curious, Gunnar wears number 29 in honor of Marc-Andre Fleury, the best-ever goalie for my beloved Pittsburgh Penguins.

ALSO BY LAINEY DAVIS

Stag Brothers Series

Sweet Distraction (Tim and Alice)

Filled Potential (Ty and Juniper)

Fragile Illusion (Thatcher and Emma)

A Stag Family Christmas

Beautiful Game (Hawk and Lucy)

Stag Generations Books

Forging Passion (Wes and Cara prequel)

Forging Glory (Wes and Cara)

Forging Legacy (Wyatt and Fern)

Forging Chaos (Odin and Thora)

Playing for Keeps (Gunnar and Emerson)

Playing for Payback (Alder and Lena)

Playing for Power (Tucker and …)

Bridges and Bitters series

Fireball: An Enemies to Lovers Romance (Sam and AJ)

Liquid Courage: A Marriage in Crisis Romance (Chloe and Teddy)

Speed Rail: A Single Dad Romance (Piper and Cash)

Last Call: A Marriage of Convenience Romance (Esther and Koa)

Planted and Plowed series

Against the Grain (Eila and Ben)

The Burgh and the Bees (Eden and Nate)

Yule Be Sorry (Eliza and ???)

Sappy Go Lucky (Eva and Asher)

Since You've Bean Gone (Ethan and Lia) *part of the Farm 2 Forking series

Binge the following series in eBook, paperback, or audio!

Brady Family Series

Foundation: A Grouchy Geek Romance (Zack and Nicole)

Suspension: An Opposites Attract Romance (Liam and Maddie)

Inspection: A Silver Fox Romance (Kellen and Elizabeth)

Vibration: An Accidental Roommates Romance (Cal and Logan)

Current: A Secret Baby Romance (Orla and Walt)

Restoration: A Silver Fox Redemption Romance (Mick and Celeste)

Oak Creek Series

The Nerd and the Neighbor (Hunter and Abigail)

The Botanist and the Billionaire (Diana and Asa)

The Midwife and the Money (Archer and Opal)

The Planner and the Player (Fletcher and Thistle)

Stone Creek University

Deep in the Pocket: A Football Romance

Hard Edge: A Hockey Romance

Possession: A Football Romance